# Katy's Pony Summer

# Katy's Pony Summer

Victoria Eveleigh

*Illustrated by Chris Eveleigh*

Orion
Children's Books

Orion Children's Books

First published in Great Britain in 2016
by Hodder and Stoughton

3 5 7 9 10 8 6 4 2

A CIP catalogue record for this book
is available from the British Library.

ISBN: 978 1 4440 1453 2

Printed and bound in Great Britain by Clays Ltd, St Ives plc

The paper and board used in this book are
made from wood from responsible sources.

Orion Children's Books
An imprint of
Hachette Children's Group
Part of Hodder and Stoughton
Carmelite House
50 Victoria Embankment
London EC4Y 0DZ

An Hachette UK Company

www.hachette.co.uk
www.hachettechildrens.co.uk

For Meghan, our first grandchild,
who was born as I was writing this story.

# Exmoor

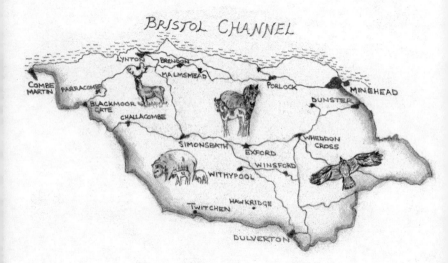

BRISTOL CHANNEL

LYNTON · BRENDON
MALMSMEAD
COMBE
MARTIN · PARRACOMBE · PORLOCK · MINEHEAD
DUNSTER
BLACKMOOR
GATE
CHALLACOMBE
WHEDDON
CROSS
SIMONSBATH · EXFORD
WINSFORD
WITHYPOOL
HAWKRIDGE
TWITCHEN
DULVERTON

# Meet the ponies . . .

### Trifle

Trifle is a registered Exmoor mare. She was born on the moorland above Barton Farm on Katy's birthday, and from the moment Katy saw her she knew they were destined to be together. Since then they've had plenty of adventures together.

### Tinkerbell

Tinkerbell (Tinks for short) is Trifle's foal who arrived unexpectedly just before Christmas. Katy reckons she was the best Christmas present ever!

## Jacko

Jacko is a liver chestnut Welsh cob gelding. He's 14 hands (142 centimetres) high, and is a fun, reliable all-rounder. Katy loved him from the moment she started riding him at Stonyford Riding Stables, and she couldn't believe her luck when her Granfer bought him for her as a surprise birthday present. There's nothing Katy and Jacko enjoy more than riding over Exmoor, with a few good gallops along the way.

## Max

In his prime, Max was Melanie's top-class show hunter. He's a stunning 17 hands (173 centimetres high) chestnut gelding, and he's very well schooled. Melanie only allows a few people to ride him, including Alice.

# Contents

# 1

# The Intruders

In a perfect world it would always be summer, Katy decided as she led Trifle, her Exmoor pony, across the field. Everything was easier – even simple stuff like being able to wear a T-shirt and shorts all day long.

With nearly four weeks to go before school started again, most of the holidays lay ahead, crammed with things she and her friend Alice were planning to do, from a beach barbecue to Exmoor Pony Festival events and, best of all, a camping trip on horseback.

The girls had been planning their trip for ages. They'd done a long-distance ride over Exmoor a couple of years ago with Alice's mum and twin brothers, but this time it would just be the two of them and they'd be camping in a tent rather than sleeping in proper beds. The route they'd take would be similar, though, and they'd be staying at Mrs Soames' farm near Withypool. They'd be like proper travellers from times gone by, living with their horses day and night . . .

Insects buzzed around Katy's head, reminding her that hot weather came at a price, but she hardly noticed them.

Trifle grabbed her attention by grinding to a halt, head up and ears pricked.

Squinting against the mid-morning sun, Katy could just make out a group of red deer concealed in the lush grass of Moor Field.

Trifle always became agitated when she saw deer. Perhaps it was because they reminded her of when she was an untamed foal running free on the moor. Granfer, who'd spent a lifetime on Exmoor, said ponies and deer had a lot in common and seemed to understand one another. Well, these had certainly rekindled Trifle's wild nature, which wasn't ideal under the circumstances. Katy and Alice were trying to train Trifle and her eight-month-old foal, Tinks, to walk away from each other calmly, and at that moment Alice and Tinks were coming back, having gone round the field in the opposite direction. It had all been going amazingly well, until now.

2

Katy adjusted her grip on the lead rope. Her free arm pointed at the gate, wiggled her head in an attempt to mime antlers, to her lips and indicated down the hill towa home, hoping Alice would realise it meant *let's walk away quietly because there are deer in the field*.

"What's the matter?" Alice called.

"Shhh!" Katy hissed, but it was too late. First one, then two, then all of the stags leapt up, their velvet-clad antlers bobbing along as they fled back to the open moorland. Within a few seconds they'd sprung onto the far hedgebank and away out of sight.

Trifle's head craned even higher, and her eyes bulged with excitement. She pranced around, shaking her head whenever she felt the lead rope's restraint. Katy held on with both hands and talked to her in a soothing voice.

Alice came closer, and Trifle's attention turned to her foal, greeting her with affectionate mutterings.

Tinks had been a lot less bothered about their separation. Unlike her mum, she'd been domesticated from birth. She'd always been self-assured, and seemed as happy with people as she was with ponies.

"Why the game of charades?" Alice asked.

"I was *trying* to show there were lots of stags in the field."

Alice hurried towards the gate. "Ooh! Where?"

"Too late. They went when they heard your voice."

"Ah. Sorry."

"Don't worry. They weren't supposed to be in there anyway. Dad was planning to cut for silage soon, so he won't be pleased about the damage to the grass."

Trifle's dark nostrils sifted the air, picking up messages no human could detect, and her hazelnut eyes scanned the brow of the hill where the hedge against the Common curled out of sight. She let out a resounding neigh.

With a thud of unshod hooves, a band of Exmoor ponies cantered into view. The ponies sped towards the gate, peeled away at the last moment and regrouped, trampling swathes of grass in the process.

Trifle and Tinks stood side by side, bristling with tension.

There were four mares, two yearlings and four foals. Katy knew most of the individuals by sight, even though they all looked similar: brown bodies, dark manes and tails, typical Exmoor mealy markings and not a white hair between them.

She could understand how the deer had got into the field – they could jump almost any hedge or fence on Exmoor, giving them the freedom to go where they pleased – but the ponies were different. They weren't in the habit of jumping to and fro. In fact, the only other time they'd broken into Moor Field was during a stormy night nearly two years ago when the gate onto the Common had been damaged. The whole herd had come in and feasted on some silage bales that Tom was supposed to have fenced off.

But this wasn't the whole herd. Why were there so few of them? And they seemed unsettled. It didn't feel right.

An urgent whinny came from the direction of the Common. The ponies wheeled round and charged back over the horizon.

Tinks plunged forward in an attempt to follow, then reared up in frustration as she felt the tug of her lead rope.

Katy held her breath, watching helplessly as the filly looked as if she might go over backwards, but Alice averted disaster by letting the lead rope go slack so there was nothing to pull against. Tinks landed the right way up and stood still, legs trembling. Alice used the window of opportunity to shorten the rope again and lead her in circles, stopping every now and then to back up a few steps. Katy had seen her use similar tactics when riding highly-strung horses; it released their pent-up energy and gave them something else to think about. Thank goodness for Alice, she thought, and copied what she was doing to calm Trifle too.

"All that horse agility training was so useful," Alice said. "She wouldn't have calmed down nearly as quickly at the beginning of the holidays, would she?"

"Trifle wouldn't have either," Katy agreed. "It's made her so much easier to control from the ground, even when she gets super-excited."

They'd spent the first weeks of the summer holidays preparing for a horse agility fun day organised by Alice's stepfather, Dean. The things they'd practised had taught them a lot about horsemanship.

"At least James wasn't riding Trifle," Alice said. "Pure luck he's gone to see his grandparents today."

Katy nodded, but her mind was on the ponies and how they'd got into the field. "I'd love to go in and see whether the gate onto the Common's open, but I don't dare with these two in tow."

Alice held out her hand. "I'll stay here with them, if you like."

Katy hesitated. It would be unfair to expect Alice to deal with both Trifle *and* Tinks. "Thanks, but we'll need some help to get those mares and foals back onto the Common where they belong, and we can't do it leading these two. We'd better go back home and find someone." She looked at the haphazard maze of flattened grass in the field. "I dread to think what Dad will say when he sees this. Exmoor ponies aren't his favourite creatures at the best of times."

*

The girls put Trifle and Tinks back into their stable, next to Jacko, and hurried to the farmhouse. A smart four-wheel-drive vehicle was parked outside.

Must be some bed and breakfast people, Katy thought, but as soon as she walked into the kitchen she realised it wasn't. "Sharon!" she cried. "What are you doing here?"

Sharon got up from the kitchen table and hugged her. "That's a fine way to greet an old friend," she said. Even though she'd left Ireland years ago, her voice still had an Irish lilt to it.

"I mean it's a lovely surprise! I haven't seen you for *ages* – except the Fun Day, of course, but we hardly had time to speak then." Katy hugged her friend again, noticing she was as skinny as ever. She also appeared to have shrunk, but maybe that was because Katy had grown taller.

Sharon grinned. "Sorry, I know I've been rubbish at keeping in touch. Time's just flown by. It's been hectic at the stables, what with Rachel going part-time and all, *and . . .*" she stretched her arm out to the young man sitting at the kitchen table, "Adam and I have been pretty busy getting to know each other."

Adam came over, towering above Sharon as he put a protective arm around her shoulder.

"Great to meet you at last, Katy," he said. "Sharon's told me so much about you."

"Oh dear," Katy said. So this was Sharon's vet! Rachel had said he was good-looking, and she was right.

He smiled. "Not 'oh dear' at all. She says you've been like a younger sister to her since she moved to Exmoor."

Katy remembered when she and Sharon had agreed to adopt each other as sisters. Was it nearly two years ago? Such a lot had happened since then.

Sharon hugged Alice and introduced her to Adam before saying, "In fact, you good people are the closest thing I have to family, which is why I wanted to tell you our news." She beamed. "We're engaged to be married!"

In the general commotion of kissing, hugging and congratulating that followed, Dad opened some sparkling wine and Tom found champagne glasses while Mum made what she called "nibbles" but most people would have called a meal.

At last there was a lull in the conversation. Katy knew she had to tell Dad about the ponies, even if it spoiled the party. "Er, Dad?"

"Yes, me darling?" he replied light-heartedly.

"You know Moor Field?"

He looked amused. "Ye-es."

"Well, several ponies have got in there somehow. Alice and I couldn't do anything about them because we had Trifle and Tinks with us, but perhaps we ought to get them out?"

"Typical! They could have waited until we'd cut the

grass." Dad looked at Sharon and Adam apologetically. "Why don't you stay and talk to Sally while Tom and I help the girls? We shouldn't be long."

Sharon pushed back her chair and stood up. "We'll come too. It'll be fun."

"*Nothing* to do with Exmoor ponies is *ever* fun," Dad said. "Okay, then. Tom can take the quad bike and we'll go up in the Land Rover."

D ad drove the Land Rover, Mum sat in the passenger seat and Katy, Alice, Sharon and Adam sat on the cramped seats in the back, their legs bumping against each other as they drove over ruts baked hard by the summer sun. Katy remembered how she used to love riding in the back like this. It had seemed a huge adventure. Now it was plain uncomfortable. She had to lean forward to prevent her head from banging against the window and, looking down, she couldn't help comparing her legs with Alice's beautiful sun-tanned ones.

Dad parked the Land Rover outside the gate into Moor Field, and they all spilled out. He swore under his breath when he saw the ponies and the trampled grass. "The sooner we get those four-legged locusts out of here, the better. Somebody can't have shut the gate properly. Is it still open?"

Mum went to check, while Dad organised the troops, sending Katy and Alice to the left while Sharon and Adam went to the right and he and Tom covered the centre ground.

The ponies ran up the hill, through the gate and onto the Common like sand slipping through an hourglass.

"Well, that was easier than expected," Tom said.

Sharon grinned. "Many farmhands make light work, see?"

"It was shut, by the way," Mum said, latching the gate and tying it with baler twine for good measure.

They all agreed that somebody must have seen the open gate and, trying to be helpful, had shut it, trapping the ponies on the wrong side.

A lone Exmoor mare trotted over the hill with rigid, hesitant steps, caught sight of everybody and hurried away again.

Dad sighed. "There's always one. She'll be much harder to get out on her own, but I really don't want to bring the others back again. You stay here as gate monitor, Sal, and we'll see if we can gently guide her along the hedge."

Swishing through the long grass, they spread out in a shallow arc as they walked upwards, hoping to guide the pony back to the gate.

Eventually Katy spotted her standing by the hedge at the top of the field. She'd sensed their advance, and started moving downhill in the right direction. They followed her from a distance, careful not to panic her. If she became frightened she'd go too fast and miss the open gate. Their method seemed to be working, but all of a sudden the mare wavered, turned round and hurried back to where she'd been before, nickering repeatedly.

"Hang on, I think she might have a foal hidden in the grass up there," Katy said.

She walked on alone, trying to see if she could identify the pony. Yes, she was certain now: the mare was unmistakably Trifle's mum, Tormentil. Katy knew she'd had a colt foal this year because she'd seen him on the Common several times. Alice had singled him out as the foal she'd love to buy if she could take her pick. But where was he now? There didn't appear to be anything in the grass, and Tormentil was much more interested in the hedgebank – which was mostly bank, with some patchy gorse on top like an untidy hairstyle. A double-stranded wire fence had been set at an angle near the top on each side to discourage animals from attempting to climb over. Tormentil pawed at its base, turned to Katy and then pawed again.

As Katy moved closer there was an abrupt snagging noise from the far side of the hedgebank, and some gorse branches rustled violently. Trying to avoid pulling down the wire fence, Katy scrabbled halfway up the bank to take a better look. Her bare limbs felt every stone, root, nettle and thorn, but she forgot her discomfort as soon as she caught sight of what lay on top.

A foal's head, white-eyed with fear, stared back at her. He struggled, and the peculiar snagging noise started up again, causing mini-shockwaves through the hedge.

Katy parted the dense, prickly branches: one of the foal's hind legs was caught in a twist of wire from the fence on the moorland side of the bank. The wire had become wrapped around his cannon bone, just below the hock. Every time he moved, it cut a little deeper into his limb. There was surprisingly little blood, but somehow that made the wound more sinister. Flies swarmed in the midday heat. The coconut smell of the gorse flowers, which Katy usually loved, became sickly-sweet all of a sudden.

Panic swelled inside her, making it hard to breathe. "Help!" she shouted, waving frantically. "Over here!"

# 2

# Time and Money

It soon became clear that it would be easier to rescue the foal from the other side. So they all moved round, leaving the mare fretting in the field by herself.

Tom found some wire-cutters in the toolbox on the quad bike, and held the foal as still as possible while Adam freed the foal's leg.

As soon as he was free from the wire and down on the ground, the foal tried to run away. Tom and Dad held on to him, one on each side, and everyone fell silent while Adam assessed the damage.

From the way the colt was standing, Katy could see

there was something seriously wrong. He couldn't put any weight on his damaged leg, and the toe of his hoof bent over and dragged along the ground.

"I'm afraid it doesn't look good," Adam said. "His extensor tendon is exposed, and there must be significant damage because there's no movement in his foot."

"Roughly translated, that means what?" Tom asked.

Adam gave him a rueful smile. "It means I'm really sorry, but it would probably be the kindest thing to put him down as soon as possible."

"I'll go and get the gun," Tom said. Adam took Tom's job of holding the foal while he went off on the quad bike.

Katy stared after her brother's receding back. How could such a big decision be made so quickly? "*Probably* means there's an element of doubt," she said to Adam. "So there must be at least one other option."

"Theoretically, yes," he replied carefully, "but it wouldn't be practical – not for a wild foal like this."

The flicker of hope inside her became a flame. "Why not?"

"Because treating him is bound to be stressful for all concerned, and even after weeks of nursing, his foot may never work properly again. Also, of course, there's the time and money involved."

"How much?" Katy knew she was being rude

interrogating him like this, but it really was a matter of life and death.

"I'm afraid that's a bit like asking, 'How long is a piece of string?'" Adam replied. "The answer is, I don't know, but a lot of both."

"Far too much, anyway," Dad said, coming to his rescue.

So that was it! "Why is *everything* about money?" Katy asked, her voice high with indignation. "How can you put a price on a life?"

"Farmers have to do it all the time, love," Dad replied gently. "You know that as well as anyone."

Katy felt as if she was swimming against the tide and the tide was winning. It had happened to her once down at the beach. She'd been convinced she'd die, and had been frightened of water ever since. Swimming pools were bad enough, but the sea was terrifying. She could still remember what that level of panic felt like – it would stay with her forever. A lifeguard had rescued her, thank goodness.

Well, today she had to be the foal's lifeguard; he'd die if she didn't throw him a lifeline. "Ponies aren't like cattle and sheep," she insisted. "And this one's Trifle's little brother, so that makes him extra-special."

"How can you be so sure?" Dad asked.

Katy pointed in the direction of the mare in the field. "She's Tormentil, Trifle's mum, and this year she had

15

a dark colt foal with a double whorl on his forehead. I saw him just after he was born, and I've been keeping an eye on him ever since. He's perfect – everything a future stallion should be." She glanced at the broken creature, and forced back hot tears as she remembered how flawless and full of life he'd been.

Adam inspected the foal's head. "Two whorls. How unusual." He looked at Katy. "Do you know all the members of the herd by sight?"

"Pretty much." This conversation is going off-track, she thought desperately. Soon Tom will return with the gun.

"Katy's completely nuts about her Exmoors," Alice said. "She owns them, you see. Granfer gave them to her."

Adam seemed to regard Katy with new respect. "Wow, quite a responsibility."

"Yes, that's just it!" she said, seizing the opportunity. "I feel responsible for this foal, which is why I want to do everything I can to save him, even if it does take a lot of time and money."

Dad raised his eyebrows.

"My time, my money," she added firmly before he could say anything.

"Are you sure about this?" Adam asked.

Katy sensed she was winning. "Completely sure," she said emphatically.

"If this foal does recover – and it's a big *if* – the cost could amount to quite a sum, you know," he warned. "Far more than he's worth."

"Exmoor ponies are always more trouble than they're worth," Dad said.

Katy was indignant. "How about Trifle? She saved the farm *and* Granfer's life!"

"Hm, Trifle's the exception that proves the rule," Dad replied with a hint of a smile.

"I'll help Katy look after him," Alice said to Adam. "It'll be great practical experience. I want to be an equine vet, you see."

"Good for you," he said. "I can guarantee you'll get plenty of bandaging practice, anyway." He looked from the girls to Mum and Dad, and back again. "If we *are* going to give him a chance, we need to act quickly. The main thing is to keep his wound moist so the tendon doesn't dry out, and also as clean as possible. Then, before we move him, I'll need some sort of absorbent dressing and some clean bandages. Oh, and honey would be good, if you've got any."

Fired up with enthusiasm, Katy said, "I've got a poultice left over from treating Jacko's abscess, and some stable bandages. A couple of tail bandages too, if you need them."

"I'm sure we've got some of those special non-stick dressings in the first aid box. And there's plenty of honey," Mum added. "I give it to the bed and breakfast guests."

"Ideal," Adam said. "Right now, I really need to keep this wound damp. Did I see a bottle of water in the back of the Land Rover?"

"I'll check," Mum said, and hurried away to take a look.

Dad sighed. "So we're going for plan B – expense, hassle and heartache – are we?"

Katy hugged him. "Yes, but you won't need to do a thing, I promise."

Adam, Sharon, Katy and Alice took it in turns to hold the colt and splash his wound with water at regular intervals while Katy's parents drove home to get supplies for Tom to bring up with the tractor and link box.

Katy could feel her bare skin cooking in the midday sun. When she held the foal, his fur felt clammy against her hands. Sweaty patches spread from his belly and neck like an incoming tide, gradually wetting his entire body. His neck drooped and he stopped struggling.

Flies homed in, crawling and buzzing.

*Come on, Tom! Come on!*

At last he arrived.

Adam spread honey over the open wound, put

a dressing on top and bandaged it in place. Then he bandaged the whole lower leg to hold the foal's foot firmly in the correct position before they manhandled him into the link box. It was obvious he was really stressed and in a lot of pain.

Katy felt so sorry for him, but told herself he'd soon recover once he was safely in the shed with his mum. All they had to do was get them both home.

They positioned him with his head looking outwards – Sharon and Katy on one side and Adam and Alice on the other – hoping that Tormentil would follow as they drove away. It wasn't easy; the link box jolted and swayed over the rock-hard ground. Tormentil trailed behind, as if joined by an invisible thread, but about halfway across the field the thread was broken and she stood in an agony of indecision before fleeing back to the gate onto the Common where the herd was waiting for her.

Tom turned the tractor around.

"Drive slower next time, Tom!" Katy shouted through the rear window of the tractor.

"If I drive too slowly it'll give her time to think about joining her friends on the moor," he replied. "Don't look her in the eye, or you'll scare her away for certain."

"I'm not completely stupid," Katy retorted.

"Matter of opinion."

"Good to know nothing's changed in my absence," Sharon said. "You two are priceless when you get going."

Tom grinned at her, shifted the tractor into low range and set off at a snail's pace.

Despite their best efforts, Tormentil lost her nerve even more quickly.

Tom had an "I told you so" look on his face. "I reckon there are too many of you in the link box," he said.

Katy hated to admit it, but he was probably right. The more people there were, the more frightened Exmoor ponies could become. "Tell you what, Alice," she said, "I'll go this way and you go over there. We'll walk around behind her and then follow at a safe distance so she won't be tempted to double back."

It was a good plan that should have worked, but Tormentil was so worried about keeping an eye on the two girls shadowing her that she hardly looked at her foal at all. Soon her flight instinct kicked in and she bolted away, head down, legs like pistons, heading for the gate at the top of the field yet again.

"It's no good, we'll have to let her out onto the Common," Adam said. "Top priority is to get this little chap home before it's too late."

"Will he survive without his mum?" Katy asked.

"I'm afraid we haven't got much choice. Weaning at

four months isn't ideal, but he's well-grown. It won't be possible to train him to a bottle now, but he should be okay with foal milk pellets, forage and water."

"How expensive are the pellets?"

"Not cheap," Adam admitted.

Sharon and Adam stayed with the foal while the girls manoeuvred Tormentil towards the gate and Tom kept the herd at bay on the moor.

"I feel awful about taking her baby away from her, but it'll make things simpler, I suppose," Katy said as she and Alice climbed back into the link box. "Tormentil would have hated being in the shed. She's one of the wildest mares we've got, and she's never been split from the herd. Poor little thing, though. Everything's stacked against him, isn't it? He won't even have his mum to comfort him now. If only we'd found him sooner!"

Alice stroked the foal's back. "Well, it's lucky we found him when we did."

"That's true enough," Sharon agreed. "Look on the bright side."

But Katy couldn't. The triumph she'd felt about saving the foal's life ebbed away, replaced by a creeping doubt that maybe she hadn't done the right thing after all.

# 3

# Bandages

By the time they got back to the farm, Dad had cleaned a small pen in the sheep shed and bedded it up with straw.

Tom backed the tractor into the shed, and they pushed the foal gently into the pen. Once in there he didn't charge around, as Katy had been afraid he would. He just stood still with his head near the ground and his eyes half closed, shivering.

"Is he okay?" Katy asked anxiously.

"It's a pity this happened on such a hot day," Adam said, which wasn't the reassurance she'd been hoping for. "He's bound to be in shock, and badly dehydrated."

Katy had an idea. "Trifle's still feeding her foal, even though Tinks is eight months old now. She'll have milk! Perhaps she'll let this foal suckle her too. After all, he is her brother."

Adam smiled at her kindly. "Not a chance, I'm afraid."

"But people do adopt foals onto mares, like we do with ewes and lambs," Katy protested. "I'm sure I've read about it."

"Yes, it's perfectly possible with a newborn foal and a mare that's lost her own foal of a similar age, but another thing entirely with a four-month-old foal and a mare who's still suckling her foal of eight months."

"Oh." Katy felt deflated. It had seemed such a brilliant solution.

"Now then, let's make a better job of cleaning the wound and bandaging this chap's leg properly," Adam said. "We'll also need some disinfectant, cotton wool and warm water."

"I'll go," Alice said.

"I'll come with you," Sharon offered, and they sprinted to the farmhouse together.

Katy stood by the foal's pen with Adam. "Thanks for all your help," she said awkwardly.

"I've hardly done anything," he replied. "The real

work's yet to come, I'm afraid. For a start, the dressings will need to be changed twice a day. If I show you how, will you be able to do it after that?"

*No way!* Katy had assumed that the present bandage would stay on until Adam could come and change it. The thought of having to deal with that gruesome wound and floppy hoof all by herself filled her with horror. She'd been taught about first aid bandages at Pony Club, of course, but they'd just practised on tame ponies that had had nothing wrong with them. This was real and super-scary. Yet how could she say she wouldn't be able to do it when she'd insisted on saving him? She gave Adam what she hoped was an enthusiastic smile. "I'll try my best."

"It'll need to be done again this evening, then every morning and evening after that," Adam went on. "It's really important to keep the wound from drying out while the tendon's exposed like this, and vital to make sure everything is as clean as possible. All being well, as the skin heals the tendon will heal underneath. If it doesn't, his foot will always be floppy and useless."

Katy found it hard to concentrate. Her brain felt scrambled. The instructions kept coming.

"If his leg becomes at all smelly, that's a sign of infection, and infection's bad news. If possible, leave the bandages off for a few minutes every time you change them, just to let the skin breathe, and watch out for pressure sores. Attention to detail is really important."

"Yes, I can see that." Katy hoped she sounded dependable.

"While we're waiting, a bucket of water for the little chap would be good," Adam said. "The sooner he drinks, the better. Make sure both the bucket and the water are clean. He'll be used to drinking from streams, so if it smells strange it may put him off."

Katy fetched a bucket, rinsed it, scrubbed it and rinsed it again before filling it from the trough in the yard, which was fed by rainwater.

"Make sure it's full to the brim," Adam called. "Nervous horses won't eat or drink from anything unless they can see at the same time."

The bucket was so full that Katy struggled with the weight and found it impossible not to slop cold water down her legs and into her shoes.

"Sorry, I should be doing that," Adam said, taking it from her and carrying it to the pen.

The foal stood there, trembling slightly.

Alice arrived with a container of warm water, a bowl, disinfectant and a packet of cotton wool.

Sharon followed, carrying a shopping bag from which she pulled a couple of flasks, plastic cups and a container of sandwiches. She handed round cups of ice-cold lemonade. "Needless to say, Sally wouldn't let us out of the kitchen without food and drink."

Katy drank a whole cupful in one go, relishing the feeling of the cool liquid soothing her parched throat. "You know what Mum's like," she said. "If it stands still, dust it; if it moves, feed it."

They all laughed, and Sharon raised her cup. "Good on your mum. She's one in a million."

After their short lunch break they set to work. Sharon held the foal and Alice handed things to Adam while he helped Katy to take off the first bandage, clean the wound with disinfectant, apply a wound dressing, secure it in place and then bandage the whole leg firmly so the foal's foot was held in the correct position.

Even with so many assistants, Katy felt as if she didn't have enough hands. It didn't help that the colt tried to kick whenever he felt anything touching his injured leg.

The old bandage was gooey with pus. She was beginning to see why they'd need a lot of bandages and dressings. "How long will I have to do this for?" she asked.

"About four weeks for the whole leg," Adam replied. "By then his foot should begin to function again if the tendon's healing properly."

Four weeks! Katy thought. Nearly a month until they'd find out whether it had all been worthwhile.

At the end of the summer holidays they'd know.

"But you'll have to keep the actual wound covered for longer – until the skin heals over completely," Adam said. "Six to eight weeks, at a guess, if all goes well. I can't stitch anything because of the risk of infection. It must heal from the inside out."

*Six to eight weeks!*

"Bandages are often one of the major expenses with this sort of job, but it's possible to improvise, especially with a small leg like this. Your mum does bed and breakfast in the farmhouse, doesn't she?"

Katy nodded, wondering where on earth this was leading.

"Has she got any old sheets? Ones that are too worn for the guests?"

"Yes, there's a whole shelf of them in the airing cupboard."

"Excellent," Adam said. "The bandage we've just put on was about the right length and width, so you can cut some old sheets to approximately the same size and use them instead. Much cheaper, just as effective and you needn't feel guilty about chucking everything away afterwards."

Sharon looked at her watch. "Jeepers, we'll have to go soon, Adam, if you're on call this evening."

"Sorry! I didn't realise," Katy said. "You haven't exactly had a day off, have you?"

27

Sharon grinned. "Not to worry. It's been great to help."

"I'm really sorry, but I've got to go too," Alice said. "I promised Mum I'd get home in time to lead a pony in the four o'clock beginners' ride."

"We'll give you a lift," Sharon offered. "Save you having to walk. We'll be going past the entrance to Stonyford anyway."

"Great. Thanks."

"I'll drop in when I can tomorrow to see how this little chap is and give him a couple of tetanus jabs," Adam said to Katy. "I'll see if I can get some antibiotic paste, too. It'll be easier to give something by mouth than inject him day after day. Make sure the bandage stays in place, and encourage him to eat and drink."

"What should I give him to eat?" It seemed an odd question to ask, but Katy wasn't sure about anything anymore.

"Fresh-cut grass to start with. Then, once he's eating something familiar, you can introduce other food like hay and foal pellets. Pieces of apple will be good, too."

"Okay," Katy said, thinking, *Help! I don't think I can do this!*

The shed was eerily quiet when everyone had gone.

Four weeks of bandaging and minimal movement, Adam had said. Only then would they have some idea about whether the foal would be permanently lame or not.

And then what?

If he turned out to be unsound, nobody would want him. Even if his foot was okay, it would be a long haul to get him completely right and he'd probably always have a scar, which could also mean nobody would want him.

She hadn't thought it through properly – hadn't realised what would be involved, for him or for her. Had she condemned him to a fate worse than death? Would he have to be put down anyway?

What about the camping holiday she and Alice had planned together? They wouldn't be able to go now, thanks to her.

She swished her finger around in the bucket to show the foal there was water in it.

He flinched away.

Perhaps he'd drink if she left him alone for a while. She went out of the shed into the startling sunshine, walked up the lane a little way and started to pull handfuls of long, leafy grass from the verge.

Was this how the rest of the summer holidays would be?

If the foal survived – and she wanted him to more than anything in the world – she'd have to do whatever it took, even if it meant four weeks of worrying, changing bandages and pulling grass.

# 4

# After Dark

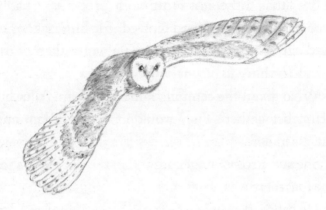

Katy couldn't sleep. It was too hot with her duvet and too cold without, but the thing that really kept her awake was worry.

After supper, Dad had held the foal still while she'd changed the bandage with fumbling fingers. It had taken ages. Even though the foal was becoming weaker, he'd still struggled and kicked.

He desperately needed to eat and drink, but it looked as if he wasn't doing either. Dad had suggested getting some water into him with a large syringe – the sort he used for injecting cattle – and it had sort of worked, even though it was clear the foal thought Katy was trying to torture him rather than save him. She'd forced herself to carry on squirting water into his mouth, regardless of the terror in his eyes. He'd never learn to trust her at this rate, and who could blame him?

She turned over, put her head on one pillow and hugged the other for comfort.

She should have picked him some fresh grass before they left. The old stuff could be going stale by now. Come to think of it, at Pony Club they'd been told never to give grass clippings to horses. She couldn't remember why exactly, but she knew colic and laminitis had been mentioned. Pulled grass was much longer than grass clippings, of course, but would it have the same effect? She imagined the foal filling up with gases like a balloon and thrashing around in the dark. The image wouldn't go away, even though she tried to tell herself it was nonsense. Adam was a fully qualified vet, so if he'd told her to pull grass for the foal then that had to be right. What if he'd got it wrong or she'd misunderstood him, though? What if he'd forgotten to say that the grass had to be kept fresh by changing it every few hours?

Unable to bear it any longer, she got up, put on some jeans and a sweatshirt, slipped her feet into her trainers, picked up her torch and went to check the foal.

*

Reality turned out to be far less dramatic but almost as worrying. The foal was facing the corner opposite the bucket of water and pile of grass, standing with his head so low to the ground that his muzzle nearly touched the straw. When Katy entered his pen his reaction was much more subdued than it had been before, but he moved away as quickly as he could when she tried to stroke him.

She lifted the bucket up so that the water made contact with his muzzle. Some of it slopped into the straw. He sneezed and turned his head away.

She remembered Granfer saying, "You can lead a horse to water but you can't make him drink." How true.

She put the bucket down, collected the fresh grass she'd picked on the way up to the shed and offered some to the foal.

He recoiled from her outstretched hand.

"Please eat!" she whispered. "You won't get better if you don't eat and drink."

In an effort to do something positive, she found the syringe, filled it with water and tried to dispense it, but without Dad to hold the foal it was hopeless. She ended up tripping over the water bucket, dropping the syringe and falling over in the straw.

Worried that she was doing more harm than good, she left him alone.

It was ten past eleven – too late to ring Granfer, Alice or Sharon for advice, and she didn't have Adam's phone number. Come to think of it, she didn't even know which veterinary practice he worked for. Mum and Dad had gone to bed. That left Tom, who'd gone to the pub, so there was no telling when he'd be back or whether he'd stay with a friend overnight. His social life was a mystery to Katy, as was his ability to start work on the farm at seven o'clock every morning, no matter what he'd been doing the night before.

She didn't know what to do. If she went back to bed she wouldn't sleep, and she'd have to get up every couple of hours to check on the foal, so she may as well stay put. If he got any worse, she'd wake her parents and call the vet, even though an out-of-hours visit would probably use up all her savings.

A huge pile of bulging woolsacks was stacked nearby, ready to be taken to the Wool Board. Katy and Alice had often said what a comfy bed a woolsack would make. Feeling rather like Goldilocks, she tried lying on them. The full ones that had been sewn up were too bulging and firm, but one – the final sack to be filled, with only a few fleeces in it – was just right. She dragged it over to the foal's pen so she could be near him, and collected some empty woolsacks to use as blankets.

Her makeshift bed wasn't bad, but she couldn't relax. After the heat of the day her skin felt clammy and prickly. Creepy-crawlies scuttled over and around her, and it sounded as if there was a much larger animal – probably a rat – at the other end of the shed. A couple of barn owls shrieked at each other, and a tawny owl in the trees outside joined in, too: *screech, screech, tawit-whoo!*

She tried to pass the time thinking of possible names for the foal, so they wouldn't have to carry on calling him "the foal" or "the colt". Nothing seemed to fit. Thistle? Nutmeg? Spice? Sam? Dylan? Rocky? Bracken? Bob?

The slightest movement from the foal's pen made her get up to take a look. She longed for him to eat and drink, or at least lie down and get some proper rest, but every time she checked he was standing in the same place. Steadfast and stubborn. Typical Exmoor, she said to herself, but she had an uneasy feeling it wasn't that at all. Life had become too much for him and he was closing down. She'd seen sheep do it. Some of them couldn't take the stress of being confined in a noisy, crowded shed at lambing time. If you didn't act quickly and put them out in a field again, they'd stop eating and drinking – simply give up on life.

But what could she do? Adam had left strict instructions that the foal should move around as little as possible, so she couldn't set him free in a field.

What were the stressful things she *could* do

something about, then? She'd assumed the foal would be comforted by her presence, but now she realised it was having the opposite effect. He was used to living wild with his mother and other ponies. People were like scary aliens – especially after all the things that had happened to him recently. He needed horses, not humans, for company.

"Alright?"

A jolt shot through Katy at the unexpected sound of a man's voice. "Tom! You nearly gave me a heart attack!"

"Sorry. I saw the light on in the shed and thought I'd better investigate. A lot of stuff's being nicked from farms at the moment. People were talking about it this evening." He came closer. "How's the patient?"

"Not g-good," Katy muttered, willing herself not to burst into tears. "He w-won't eat or anything."

Tom looked into the pen. "Hm, see what you mean. On the way out, by the looks of it."

Somehow his honesty was easier to handle than glib reassurance. It confirmed she'd have to act quickly. "I've been thinking," she said.

"Bad idea, especially at this time of night."

She ignored him. "Can you help me a minute?"

Tom looked at her suspiciously. "You don't really mean a minute, do you?"

"Okay, it won't take more than an hour," Katy said,

pressing on before he could refuse. "I want to bring Jacko, Trifle and Tinks up here to keep him company. I'm sure it'll help. He's never been alone before, and he must miss his mum and the other Exmoors terribly."

"Can't it wait till morning?"

"N-no, I d-don't think he'll l-last that l-long," Katy stuttered, wobbly again all of a sudden.

"Okay, okay!" Tom said, holding his hands up as if trying to stop the unwelcome tide of emotion from sweeping towards him. "I'll help you, but where are you going to put them?" He nodded towards the horse agility equipment from Stonyford that had been taking up most of the shed all summer.

"We could move it further down, and make up three pens for the ponies at this end."

"And what are you going to make them out of?" Tom pointed at the foal's pen. "Sheep hurdles won't be big enough."

"Er, dismantle the cattle pens outside?"

"I was afraid you'd say that."

An exhausting hour later, everything was ready.

Katy and Tom walked down the hill and past the farmhouse to get the ponies from their field. They didn't need torches: a full moon beamed down from a starlit sky.

"I'll lead Dope-on-a-rope and you can deal with Tweedle-dumb and Tweedle-dumber," Tom said, taking Jacko's head collar from Katy. Being as rude as possible about her ponies had become a habit he was unlikely to break in a hurry. Katy usually retaliated with something, but at that moment she was so grateful for his help that she handed him Jacko's head collar without a word.

The ponies seemed unfazed by being caught in the middle of the night and led up to the shed where they often did horse agility, and they were much more interested in the haynets hung up in their pens than the foal in a smaller pen nearby. In fact, it was all rather disappointing.

"Ah well, you've tried your best," Tom said. "Bed."

Katy wasn't going to give up that easily. "I'll just introduce Trifle properly," she said, putting a head collar on her once more and leading her round to stand by the foal's pen.

The foal raised his head and let out the faintest high-pitched sound as Trifle touched nostrils with him. She snorted tenderly, then plunged her head over the sheep hurdle and grabbed a mouthful grass from the fresh pile Katy had put there. *Munch, munch, munch.*

"Oi! That's his, not—" She stopped mid-sentence as the foal put his head down and lipped the grass. Trifle kept munching. The foal took a few blades into his mouth and chewed them experimentally. He obviously liked what he tasted, because he went back for more.

"Can you hold Trifle a minute?" Katy asked Tom. "I need to pull more grass."

Tom sighed. "This is ridiculous," he said, but he took Trifle's lead rope. "There's the torch. Get on with it. No faffing."

Katy grabbed the torch and headed for the verge where she'd gathered grass before. It was difficult to hold the beam steady and pull grass at the same time, and she had to be quick, so she put the torch down and scrabbled around in the moonlit semi-darkness. Her hands were stung by nettles and she accidentally squished a slug between her fingers, but she ended up with an armful of grass.

When she got back to the shed, Trifle had polished off the foal's grass and washed it down with a drink of water from his bucket, leaving a swirly film of green slobber on the surface.

"Foal drank a bit, too," Tom said.

"Oh, that's *brilliant* news!"

"Little things please little minds," Tom said, but he was smiling.

At his suggestion, they moved Trifle's pen so it was as close as possible to the foal but she wouldn't be able to steal his food and new water. Her haynet was tied nearby to encourage him to follow her example and eat as much as possible.

"Well, at least that's that sorted," Tom said. He

yawned, looked at his watch and swore. "It's nearly three o'clock! Next time I see something amiss I'll ignore it and go to bed."

# 5

# Simba

Even though she was tired, Katy got up early the next morning to check on the ponies, anxious about what she would find.

Tinks greeted her with a high-pitched, demanding whinny. Jacko's welcome was more reserved – just a fluttering of his nostrils. And Trifle...Where *was* Trifle?

She hurried over to Trifle's pen. She was lying flat out, fast asleep. The foal had been lying down, too, but he scrambled awkwardly to his feet as Katy approached. She glanced at his bandaged leg, hardly daring to look too closely in case something had gone wrong, but it seemed okay. Most of his grass had gone, and his water bucket was about half full. She felt weak with relief.

Tinks pawed impatiently at the metal bars of her pen, her hoof occasionally slipping right through. She was used to being the centre of attention, and she knew how to grab it back.

"Don't do that!" Katy exclaimed. "You'll end up with a broken leg." Realising the haynets were empty, she gathered some hay from the bale she'd opened yesterday and gave some to each pony to keep them occupied for a while.

Trifle woke up and tucked into her breakfast with enthusiasm. The foal was deeply suspicious of his, so she went outside to gather some fresh, dewy grass for him.

He started to eat the grass as soon it was dropped into his pen. Progress.

Katy shivered in the early morning air. Her clothes were damp and she felt queasy, yet hungry. Perhaps food and a cup of tea would make her feel better.


After breakfast, Dad helped Katy before he set off for town.

The foal seemed to know what was going to happen as soon as he saw Katy and Dad together, and did his best to avoid capture.

Breakfast had helped to soothe Katy's churning stomach, but it hadn't worked completely, and the sight of the foal's red-raw wound, sticky with discharge, didn't improve the situation. Cleaning it was made more difficult by his vigorous attempts to kick her away.

Katy set Trifle, Tinks and Jacko loose in the field by the shed so they could stretch their legs and eat some grass before the flies became unbearable. At this time of year she usually kept them stabled during the day and turned them out at night. She'd have to change that somehow so they could keep the foal company. Maybe she could make half the shed into a sort of corral where they could move around freely.

Katy wandered back to the farmhouse in a daze, wondering how she was going to cope. There were other things she was meant to be doing as well, like getting Jacko shod and fit, and – even more urgently – teaching Tinks how to travel in a trailer so she and Trifle could go to the Exmoor Pony Festival Meet the Herds Day next week. It was all too much. For the first time she had a real insight into how difficult it was for Dad at high-stress times like lambing . . . So many life-and-death decisions, so much money at stake, so much to do. Exhausting.

A familiar-looking van drove up as Katy was about to go into the house.

"Hi, Dave," she said to the deliveryman. "Has Mum been buying things again?" Mum did a lot of her shopping online nowadays, so Dave was a regular visitor.

He grinned and handed her a parcel. "No, this one's for your dad – painting stuff, by the looks of it. Signature, please."

Katy tried her best to do a normal signature on the weird electronic screen he held out for her.

"Hear you've rescued a foal on the moor," he said.

"How d'you know that?"

Dave gave her a cheeky grin. "Ah, news travels fast round here. What happened?"

"He got caught up in the fence on top of our boundary hedge and hurt his leg."

"That's a shame. What made him climb up there in the first place?"

"No idea, really. Some ponies and stags had escaped into the field, including the foal's mum. I expect he was left behind and panicked."

"Some grockle left the gate open, most likely," Dave suggested. "Grockle" was the slightly insulting nickname some local people gave to summer visitors.

"Yes, that's what Tom and Dad think, too," Katy replied.

"The main thing is you found him and he's going to be okay."

43

"Well, it's early days but we're going to try our best to get him right."

"Good for you. Best of luck." Dave got back into his van, turned it round and waved out of the open window as he drove away.

As soon as Katy entered the farmhouse, her phone picked up the Wi-Fi signal and started to vibrate in her pocket. She dragged herself upstairs, fell onto her bed and looked at the two text messages she'd received.

One was from Alice. She was helping with a day hack from Stonyford today, but would ride Max over early tomorrow morning.

Katy replied *Great. Jacko shod. Foal OK. C U tomoz xxxx*.

The other text was from Sharon, asking after the foal and Katy replied *OK xxxx* to that as well.

Still lying fully clothed on top of her duvet, she turned onto her back and stared blankly at the shifting patterns of sunlight on her bedroom ceiling. Her mind slid slowly into neutral.

"Katy? Are you up there?" Mum's voice shattered the blissful nothingness. "James and Olivia are here! Poor James is rather upset because they couldn't find Trifle."

James! Katy felt like kicking herself. She hadn't remembered to tell his mum, Olivia, that the ponies wouldn't be in their stables as usual that morning.

Trifle had been on loan to James for just over a week now, and he was supposed to be looking after her even though she was still at Barton Farm, but Katy was so used to doing what she liked when she liked with her ponies that she was finding it hard to adjust. James had autism, and routine was especially important to him. She could imagine how upset he'd been to find an empty stable.

Katy leapt off the bed, felt dizzy, sat down again and got up more cautiously the second time. Still half asleep, she walked carefully down the stairs.

Olivia was sitting in the kitchen, having a cup of coffee with Mum. James – who always found it hard to sit still unless he was riding Trifle – was pacing around the table. A glass of milk, clearly intended for him, remained untouched.

"I'm so sorry!" Katy said as she entered the kitchen. "I forgot to tell you I'd moved the ponies up to the barn to be with the foal."

"Never mind," Olivia said. She looked exhausted. Katy remembered that James' dad, who was a helicopter pilot, had gone back overseas early that morning. Not being able to find Trifle must have been the last thing she needed.

"I minded," James declared. "I minded a lot."

Katy knew him well enough to imagine what that had been like.

Even so, he gave her a hug. She hugged him back. To begin with she'd been embarrassed by this eight-year-old boy wrapping his arms around her whenever he saw her, but now she didn't give it a second thought. The ponies seemed to accept his enthusiastic hugs too – even Trifle, who'd never been particularly cuddly with people. Thinking about the ponies, Katy realised they were still outside in the field by the barn. She ought to get them in.

"Cup of tea, love?" Mum asked. She knew Katy didn't like coffee.

"No thanks. I'll just have a glass of water and then I'll check on the ponies." Katy took a glass from the cupboard.

"Adam dropped by to give the foal some injections. He left some antibiotic paste to give him," Mum said. "He's very pleased, by the way. Said you're doing an excellent job."

"Oh." Katy was disappointed she'd missed him. She'd wanted to check she was bandaging the leg properly, and she was longing to tell him about Trifle encouraging the foal to eat and drink.

"He wrote down his email address for you, in case you had any questions. And he said it would be really helpful to have daily photos of the wound if you've got time. Such a nice man, isn't he? I'm so pleased for Sharon," Mum said, and she started telling Olivia about Sharon and how she'd ended up working for Katy's aunt, Rachel, at the Exford Stables.

"Want to come and help me get the ponies into the barn?" Katy asked James. "You can meet the little foal, too."

James went to the door immediately and put on his boots, eager to go outside.

"Can you manage?" Olivia asked.

Katy smiled. "Yes, no problem." A few weeks ago she would have found the prospect of having to look after James daunting. He often reacted to things in unexpected ways, but she'd become used to that. Trifle clearly adored him, and it was great to have another pair of hands to help with the ponies. He'd be especially useful now there was an injured foal to deal with as well. With any luck the little colt would feel an instant connection with James, just like Trifle had.

Every step was a conscious effort for Katy as they made their way up the track to the sheep shed. Her body still ached for sleep. She let James run on ahead, wondering why he always had so much energy. She'd given up worrying about him being alone with the ponies. They all knew each other so well by now.

She was nearly at the shed when there was a metallic clatter – the sort of noise usually associated with lambing time. More often than not it meant a ewe had panicked in a sheep pen and was trying to escape.

But it wasn't lambing time. The only animal in a sheep pen at the moment was the foal.

*Oh please no!* Tiredness forgotten, she sprinted the rest of the way to the shed.

It looked as if the foal had tried, but failed, to jump out of the pen. He stood precariously on his hind legs, with one of his forelegs hooked over the barrier. As Katy approached him head-on, he panicked afresh and scrambled backwards, falling over inside the pen with another heart-stopping crash. She hardly dared look in to see what damage had been done.

The bandaged leg looked okay and so did all the others, which was a minor miracle. The foal was clearly terrified, though. He lay against the corner of his pen, sides heaving, his white-rimmed eye following her every move. His water bucket had tipped over into the straw and the water trickled over the concrete floor of the shed.

James was nowhere to be seen. Eventually she found him standing by the gate outside with his arms wrapped around his head, rocking to and fro. The ponies were jostling for position on the other side, impatient to get into the shade of the shed where the flies wouldn't bother them.

"Are you okay, James?" Katy asked, even though she knew he wasn't. "What happened?"

"Scared, scared, scared," James moaned.

"What did you expect? He's a wild pony!" Katy

snapped, then instantly regretted it. She felt cross with James for frightening the foal, but even more cross with herself for assuming that just because he'd always had a special bond with Trifle he'd be fine with any pony, tame or otherwise. She gave him a hug. "Sorry. It's okay. Everything's okay." He tensed in her arms but didn't pull away. Gradually the rocking subsided.

"Come on. We'd better get these ponies in," she said at last. "I'll get their head collars on."

As soon as he was with Trifle, James became calmer. "The foal hates me," he said sadly.

"He doesn't hate you," Katy answered. "The problem is he's not used to humans. He hasn't been tamed like the other ponies have. He's just scared of you, that's all."

James became animated. "But he makes *me* scared! He's all jumpy."

She realised how silly she'd been to let him run ahead and meet the foal without her. "Is that what happened when you saw him? You both frightened each other?" she asked gently.

He nodded.

"Do you remember how frightened you felt when Moss and I met you the first time? You didn't know that Moss is a friendly sheepdog and I'm a friendly person. It took time for you to realise that, didn't it?"

"Yes. Trifle helped," James said.

Katy ran her hand over Trifle's broad back. Her

coat was sleek and a dappled conker colour. "Yes, and Trifle's been a great help with the foal as well, showing him it's safe to eat and drink. He's much calmer when she's with him. I'm sure he'll learn to trust us, with her help. But it will take a long time and lots of patience. It's been so stressful for him. I expect he thinks we're the cause of all his pain and suffering. He doesn't realise we're trying to help him." Talking about it made Katy wonder afresh whether she'd done the right thing. "I'll just put Jacko and Tinks in their pens, and then we can take Trifle to say hello to the foal. Okay?"

James nodded. "What's he called?"

"We haven't decided yet," Katy replied.

"I've got a good name! Simba!"

Why am I not surprised? Katy smiled. James was obsessed with the story of *The Lion King*. Her automatic reaction was to dismiss his suggestion, yet the more she thought about it the more she liked it. Simba was separated from his family and survived against all odds to grow from a cub to a king. He was brave, loyal and wise – a worthy leader . . . With any luck, Simba the colt would survive and grow into Simba the Exmoor stallion, with a herd of his own to look after.

"You're brilliant, James," she said. "It's the perfect name for him. We'll call him Simba."

# 6

# The Seeds of Doubt

The following morning, Katy woke to the sound of horseshoes on tarmac outside her bedroom window. It didn't sound like Jacko's hoofbeats, but he was the only shod pony at Barton Farm. She struggled out of bed and made her way to the open window to see what was going on, stumbling over trainers she'd kicked off the night before. The day was already warm and bright, and the tantalising smells and sounds coming from the kitchen below instantly told her Mum was cooking breakfast for the guests, so it had to be about eight o'clock. She'd overslept.

Alice was sitting on Max, her mum's chestnut hunter. "*There* you are!" A mischievous grin spread over her face. "I haven't woken you, have I?"

"Course not. Been up for hours," Katy said in a husky voice, tossing her unbrushed hair away from her face and trying to conceal the fact she was still in her pyjamas. "Want some breakfast?" The smell of cooking bacon was making her tummy rumble.

"Have I ever been known to turn down a Barton Farm breakfast?" Alice asked. "Where can I put Max? You know what he's like – he'll fret in a stable all by himself."

"Hang on a minute. I'll get Jacko from the barn to keep him company." Katy got dressed in record time and ran downstairs. "Alice is here for breakfast," she said to Mum as she passed through the kitchen on her way to the back door. "We'll just put Jacko and Max in the stables and then we'll be in."

"Okay, love," Mum replied as she scurried around the kitchen, assembling several different meals at the same time with expert efficiency. "Give me ten minutes."

Max and Jacko greeted each other and settled down immediately in their adjoining stables. Like their riders, they'd known each other for several years and had become good friends.

"Breakfast time," Katy said to Alice. "Come on. Mum's expecting you."

"Your mum's amazing. Mine would have a fit if she had to do a full English breakfast for up to twelve people every morning."

"But yours runs a riding stable!" Katy had always been in awe of Alice's mum, Melanie. She'd built Stonyford Riding Stables up from scratch, and she was a brilliant horsewoman.

"True, but she's a terrible cook and our house is a tip," Alice said.

"And yet your stables are immaculate."

"True. I'm just the same; I'd far rather muck out a stable than tidy my bedroom."

"Me too," Katy agreed. She suddenly realised how much she'd always taken her mum for granted. In fact, she managed the house and their farm holiday business with as much skill as Melanie ran the riding stables. She never complained – simply got on with whatever needed to be done.

After breakfast, Dad accompanied Katy and Alice to the barn to deal with Simba's leg. Alice went into keen apprentice vet mode. She studied the wound closely – something Katy tried to avoid doing – and asked lots of questions, most of which Katy couldn't answer.

Simba was fractious. Maybe it was the stress of having another person in his pen, or it could have been the extra time it took to treat his leg, but Dad had a job to hold him still. He kept making a bid for freedom at the most critical moment, grunting with all the effort he put into it.

It took them three goes, but eventually Alice managed to bandage Simba's leg and they left him to calm down.

"He's getting worse every time," Katy said in despair. "Soon we won't be able to do a thing with him. The trouble is that every time we go in the pen it's a horrible experience because we've got to hold him still and treat his leg."

"I've just read a book about a cowboy who gets wild mustangs to accept him by going into the corral and reading aloud to them. He says it's non-threatening because he's concentrating on the book rather than the horses, and it gets them used to the sound of his voice."

"That wouldn't work for me. I hate reading aloud," Katy said. She'd always found reading difficult, but hadn't discovered why until she'd gone to secondary school and a teacher there had realised she was dyslexic. Now she had extra help and was making good progress, but she still felt anxious at the thought of having to read in public.

"This wouldn't be like reading in class," Alice insisted. "Only the ponies will hear you. You can say 'rhubarb, rhubarb, rhubarb' if you like, or just sit there and talk."

"It's a good idea," Dad said. "Worth a try."

"I suppose." Katy changed the subject. "Um, Dad?"

"Y-e-s?"

"I know you're really busy because you're cutting grass in the silage fields today, but could you *possibly* tow the trailer in here so we can practise loading Tinks and Trifle ready for the Meet the Herds Day?"

"Don't want much, do you?" Dad asked, but he was smiling. "I've got to make a couple of phone calls, then I'll do it."

Katy gave him a hug. "You're the best dad ever."

The girls decided to go for a ride on Jacko and Max straight away. The day was promising to be one of the hottest of the summer, so they headed for the open moor of the Common where there was usually a breeze to cool them down and keep the flies at bay.

Jacko had been off work for about a week, but it felt longer than that somehow. So much had happened in the past few days.

To begin with Katy insisted on taking things slowly, anxiously looking out for the slightest sign of lameness, but after a while she relaxed and enjoyed the ride. Jacko strode out purposefully with his neck arched and ears pricked, delighted to be having fun again. His enthusiasm was infectious – instant happiness. If you could bottle that feeling you'd make a fortune, Katy decided.

As they made their way home they passed some ponies. One of them was Tormentil. She raised her head briefly to look at the riders, then carried on grazing.

"That's a relief," Katy remarked. "She looks completely settled now, doesn't she?"

"Totally," Alice agreed. "Just getting on with life."

"I wish Simba would be as sensible."

"At least he's eating and drinking now."

"I suppose," Katy said. "He won't touch the special feed pellets Dad bought him yesterday, though."

"Give him time; there's so much he's got to get used to," Alice replied. "Canter to the gate?"

Katy grinned. "Okay."

The horses set off eagerly, and everything else was forgotten as they sped along side by side. Eventually they came to a juddering last-minute halt by the gate into Moor Field.

Katy automatically opened it with Jacko. Max was so tall that it was difficult for Alice to reach down far enough.

"Something's made a terrible mess of the hedge back there," Alice said as Katy secured the gate again.

"Where?"

"On the moorland side of the hedge, near the corner.

The bank's been gouged out. It's all bare earth and non-existent fencing. Didn't you see?"

"No, I was too busy trying to stop in time." Katy looked along the top hedge of Moor Field, and pointed at the place where the stags had made their escape. It was marked by a hollow, known as a rack, that had been eroded into the bank by their hooves. "The deer have made quite a mess on this side, too." She glanced at her watch. "We'd better hurry. James will have arrived by now, and I'm worried about him and Simba."

But her fears were unfounded. Once they'd settled Jacko and Max into the stables, they walked up to the barn to find James grooming Trifle in her pen with the large, soft body brush Olivia had bought him. The little mare stood with her head low, floppy-eared and floppy-lipped, blissfully soaking up the attention.

Olivia was sitting on the woolsack, reading. She always had a book with her, but rarely got a chance to read it.

Simba was lying down, despite the fact there were humans around. Nobody was paying attention to him, which must have been a refreshing change.

"I've got an important job for you and Trifle," Katy said to James. "Can you help us teach Tinks to walk into a trailer?"

He nodded his head enthusiastically. "Yes."

Olivia looked up. "Is this one of your horse agility exercises?"

"Not exactly," Katy said, realising she hadn't told her about Monday yet. This loan agreement was proving to be much more complicated than she'd imagined. "Er, I hope you don't mind, but I've agreed to take Trifle and Tinks to the Meet the Herds Day on Monday. The idea is that visitors and people planning to buy a pony can see the differences between various moorland herds and talk to the owners about the ponies they've got for sale."

James looked alarmed. "No! Not for sale!"

Katy wished she'd chosen her words more carefully. "Don't worry, Trifle and Tinks aren't for sale. It's just that they're the only tame Exmoor ponies we've got."

"They'll be ambassadors for the Barton herd," Alice added.

James looked puzzled, so Katy tried to explain. "They'll show people how lovely the ponies from Barton Farm are."

"But the others are wild and scary, like Simba," James said.

He had a point. "Ah, but that's only because they haven't been tamed. Trifle was a wild foal once, but look at her now. She's turned into a wonderful pony who trusts people," Katy said softly.

Alice had already put a head collar on Tinks and was

leading her around. They seemed to get on particularly well together, probably because Alice had set clear rules of behaviour from the start. Katy, on the other hand, had spoiled the foal when she was tiny and adorable – letting her do things she'd never allow normally, like rearing up for a titbit. As Tinks had become larger and more boisterous Katy had realised how silly she'd been, but by then the damage had been done. It was taking a long time to undo her mistakes and gain the foal's respect.

"I'll just go and let the ramp down, and scatter some straw to make it more inviting," Katy said. The only trailer they had at Barton Farm was a large metal livestock trailer, designed to transport cattle and sheep rather than horses. Everything was hard, metallic and easy to clean, with none of the safety features of horse trailers like rubber matting, padded partitions and a front ramp for unloading.

When Katy had done everything she could to make it look as appealing as possible – even putting some freshly pulled grass inside as a reward – she went back to James. "Trifle's good at loading, so if she goes in first, hopefully Tinks will follow."

"In that box?"

"Yes."

James became fidgety.

"Would you like me to lead her?" she asked.

"Yes," he replied. "I don't like boxes."

On this occasion Katy didn't try to persuade him to be brave. She didn't want James to feel left out, but she knew it would be much easier to concentrate on training Tinks if she didn't have to keep an eye on him as well, especially if Tinks panicked.

But Tinks didn't even hesitate. In the past few weeks she'd become so used to doing horse agility that the trailer must have seemed like another obstacle: up the ramp, into the box, turn round, eat grass and come out again. Lots of praise and cuddles, then do it again for fun.

"Well, that was easier than expected," Alice said, ruffling Tinks' mane. "What a good girl."

They'd set aside at least an hour for training Tinks to load, so there was time for Katy to lead James around the paddock on Trifle while Alice followed with Tinks. Before they set off they put some insect repellent on the two ponies, and it made a tremendous difference. The flies buzzed around but didn't land, so the ponies remained calm and James was happy. In fact, he became so confident that he wanted to go faster and faster.

The sun's rays felt like a physical force beating against Katy's skin. The sooner Tinks is weaned the better, she thought. Then I can lead James from Jacko, which will be much easier all round.

They turned Tinks and Trifle into the paddock and returned to the barn. "I'll just check Simba's food and water, then we can get some lunch for ourselves from the house. I don't know about you, but I could drink a whole bucketful of something cold," Katy said.

James picked up Simba's water bucket. "Here you are," he said. Sometimes it was hard to tell whether he was being funny or not.

"Thanks." She took the half empty bucket from him and pretended to drink.

James jumped up and down with glee.

"Can you go and fill this with fresh water with your mum while Alice and I pull some grass?" she asked him.

The girls soon collected a large pile of grass and took it back to Simba. He eyed them suspiciously, but began to eat as soon as they moved back a few paces.

"What shall we do about the foal pellets?" Alice asked.

"I don't know. They're so expensive, and he obviously doesn't like them." Katy rummaged around in the straw and retrieved the container, which held a mixture of dirty straw and soggy pellets. "Perhaps he'll have to survive on grass. At least he likes that."

"Make a grass sandwich," James said.

Katy wondered whether she'd heard him correctly.

"What?"

"Simba likes grass. I like sliced white bread. So make the grass into bread with new food in the middle." James looked to his mum for help.

"As you know, James loves white bread, so a good way for him to learn to eat something new is to make a sandwich of it," Olivia explained. She turned to her son. "You're suggesting they use grass like bread for a sandwich, so there's grass on the outside and pellets in the middle, aren't you? So when Simba eats the grass he'll take in a few pellets at the same time and gradually get used to them."

James nodded his head enthusiastically.

"Great idea!" Katy exclaimed. "You're a genius, James."

After they'd all had something to eat and drink in the farmhouse, Alice rode back to Stonyford on Max.

Olivia stayed in the house with Mum while James helped Katy put some fly spray on Jacko and let him out in the paddock with his friends. Then they looked in on Simba, eager to see whether the grass-and-pellet sandwich idea had worked. It had!

"Tell you what," Katy said, "Mum wants me to take some sandwiches – proper ones this time – and a flask of tea to Dad in Moor Field. D'you want to come and see the tractor at work?" James was fascinated by anything with wheels.

"Yes!" he said loudly. Simba flinched at the sudden noise. "Yes, please!"

S unny days often lost their sparkle by the afternoon and became hazy with heat, but today everything had become more intense. The sky was almost impossibly blue and the countryside shimmered with every shade of green as Katy walked up to Moor Field with Dad's lunch in a carrier bag. James ran on ahead, eager to see the tractor that they could hear already.

"Wait for me when you get to the gate!" Katy called.

By the time she'd joined him there, the tractor had just passed by with the mower humming behind it. She'd have to wait for Dad to do another circuit before she could give him his lunch.

James was mesmerised by the endless swathes of grass falling in shiny waves behind the mower. "I like wheels," he said. "Wheels and circles. I like the *Circle of Life* song, too."

"Yes, so do I," Katy said. *The Lion King* always seemed to come into their conversations somehow.

"Wheels have cool patterns," he went on. "Tractor wheels are best. They make arrows going the right way on the tyre but the wrong way on the ground."

Katy realised he was right: the pattern of a tractor tyre pointed forwards on the top part you could see, yet the imprint on the ground pointed backwards. "I'd never have thought of that. You're absolutely right."

The tractor was nearly at the brow of the hill now. Katy remembered the ponies coming over that hill, and shivered inside as she thought about finding Simba. He must have known that his mum was nearby on the other side of the hedge, panicked and jumped without thinking. She couldn't help wondering if the ponies had really come through the gate, even though everyone else thought they had. It was odd that it had been closed and secured properly. But if they hadn't come through the gate they must have jumped over the hedge somewhere, which was *really* odd. Ponies rarely attempted large obstacles like hedges unless they absolutely had to . . . She remembered what Alice had said about the damaged bank further along on the other side.

The tractor had turned the corner and was coming down the hill towards them. Katy waved and held up the plastic bag.

Dad drove to the gate and switched the engine off. The high-pitched hum of the mower became lower as the discs slowed down, then fell silent. He opened the door of the cab, jumped out and came over.

"Lunchtime!" Katy said.

"You're a star," Dad said, taking the bag from her.

"See you later." He climbed back into the cab, switched on the ignition, and drove off again.

James looked disappointed. "He didn't eat his sandwiches."

"Don't worry, he'll have them while he's going along. He can't stop because he needs to get the grass cut while the sun's hot," Katy replied.

"Oh." He gazed wistfully after the disappearing tractor.

"Tell you what . . ."

"What?"

Katy smiled. "Shall we go and see if we can find out how those ponies got into the field yesterday?"

James nodded in reply.

Together they navigated their way over the mounds of felled grass until they reached the gate onto the Common. It had been tied with baler twine for extra security.

Katy examined the ground. Confusing remnants of hoofprints, shod and unshod, marked the dry earth like the mixed-up pieces of a jigsaw puzzle. She undid the twine, unhooked the latch, walked through the gate and held it open for James.

The dusty patterns on the other side were even more difficult to decipher. Looking along the hedgebank further down the hill, she saw the place Alice had talked about, and wondered how she could have missed it. A section of hedge was missing, the wire fence had collapsed and a wide channel through the top of the bank fanned out into a crescent-shaped crater below where the soil had been worn away. It was near the corner where a neighbour's boundary hedge met theirs. This created a natural collection area they sometimes used when rounding up animals on the moor, so the plants there often looked rather trampled. Now, though, the plants appeared to have been obliterated, leaving only bare earth.

"Let's take a look over there," Katy said to James.

This particular corner of the Common often became waterlogged with rainwater running off the moor, and despite the good weather they'd had recently the ground was still slightly damp. Deer slots, unshod pony hoofprints, human footprints, some pawprints from a dog – or perhaps more than one dog – and even tyre marks were clearly visible in the soft, churned-up earth. Several deep slots confirmed that this was where the deer had been going in and out of Moor Field.

Granfer said deer had their own traditions: routes travelled, crossing places, wallows and favourite trees where they scraped the velvet off their antlers. They were creatures of habit, yet mysterious at the same time.

For as long as Katy could remember there had been

a crossing place, or deer rack, over the bank here, worn down as the deer jumped on and off to get to the other side. But this didn't look like a rack any more. It was more like a motorway under construction.

It was clear that both deer and ponies had been milling around and had broken through the bank into Moor Field at its weakest point.

Katy knew something terrifying must have happened here. She wished she could figure out what it was.

"Look," said James, pointing at a pawprint. "Odd dog."

Katy examined it. "Yes, it must have been a big dog. Or it could be a big cat – I don't know how to tell the difference." She immediately thought of the Exmoor Beast – a black panther that was rumoured to run wild on Exmoor.

"Easy," James said. "Cats don't show their claws, unless they're running or hunting."

"This animal could have been doing both," Katy said. "You're right, though, it's much more likely to be a dog. Lots of people walk their dogs up here." She studied the print closely. "Is there a bit missing? Hard to tell for sure, of course, because the ground's so churned up. It looks as if there are only three toe pads on this one. What do you think?"

James seemed exasperated by how slow she was being. "Yes, yes!"

They looked in vain for other pawprints but all the clear ones appeared to be normal.

Katy wanted to show Dad what they'd found, in case it was important, but when he came in for supper he'd already been up to the Common with Tom. They'd taken the digger, tractor, trailer and some fencing materials and had mended the hole in the hedge, which he'd noticed when he'd been cutting the grass in Moor Field.

The repair work had eradicated everything.

# 7

# Meet the Herds

The girls managed to fit in two more training sessions with Tinks and Trifle before the Meet the Herds Day. They went so well that by the time Monday arrived Katy was supremely confident both Tinks and Trifle would be a credit to the Barton herd.

She woke up with the same excited feeling she always had when going to a show, but without competition nerves. Basically, this would be a whole day of meeting friends, talking ponies and eating cake, which happened to be three of her favourite things. What could be nicer?

The ponies loaded into the livestock trailer perfectly, and soon they were on their way with Granfer driving the Land Rover and the girls in the back together. Katy could tell Granfer was excited as well because he kept up an endless stream of conversation, as if practising for the hours of chatting ahead. He'd been involved with the Exmoor Pony Society for most of his life and, even though he'd given his herd to Katy, he was still passionate about the ponies.

At Granfer's suggestion, Katy had bedded the trailer with straw and put the ponies into it loose, separated by a high partition: Trifle in the front, because she was the first to go in, and Tinks behind. This meant Tinks would be the first to come out.

Even before they let the ramp down, Katy realised she'd been over-confident about Tinkerbell's ability to behave well in public; the trailer rocked and rattled as she stormed round her small compartment, and her high-pitched whinny was impossible to ignore. Her excitement spread like wildfire to the ponies already there. Even the ones in their individual pens around the back of the building responded to her attention-grabbing neighing.

Still in high spirits, Granfer winked at Katy. "When you said you'd been training her, I didn't realise it was for a yodelling contest."

"Ha, ha, very funny." Katy tried her best to smile

even though her heart was sinking into her boots. "Let's go home. Nobody will notice."

Tinks belted out another greeting and received some enthusiastic replies.

Granfer chuckled. "I think it's safe to say the whole of Exmoor knows we're here, and everyone will notice if we leave," he said. "Courage my girl! All you've got to do is get her from the trailer to a pen and your work will be done. What could be easier than that?"

The trailer swayed violently again, rocking the Land Rover from side to side.

Granfer undid his seat belt and opened the door. "Come on. I'll get seasick if I stay in here much longer." The girls got out too, and then they all went to the back of the trailer to let the ramp down.

"Perhaps Tinks will calm down once she can see what's going on," Alice suggested.

Katy wasn't convinced. Now Tinks could hear them she'd become even more frantic.

"I'll lead her out if you like," Alice said. During the summer holidays she'd handled Tinks a lot, both walking around the farm and doing horse agility.

Katy knew she should accept Alice's offer, but pride got in the way. Granfer and all her Exmoor pony friends would be watching. She wanted to be the one to lead Tinks down the ramp for everyone to see.

"Thanks, but I'll be fine," she said, squeezing between the folding gates at the back of the trailer.

Tinks was so amazed she had company that she stood still long enough for Katy to slip a head collar on her.

"Okay!" Katy called to Granfer and Alice. "You can let me out now."

Alice opened one tailgate and Granfer opened the other.

Remembering her horse agility training, Katy stood by the filly's head with a loose rope, concentrated on where she wanted to go and stepped forwards. Breathe, she thought. I must remember to breathe.

Tinks put her front feet on the top of the ramp, hesitated for a split second and took an enormous leap onto the tarmac. Katy held onto the rope, was pulled forwards, tripped on the sloping ramp and let go as she tried to regain her balance. For a moment Tinks stood gawping, as if wondering what to do with her new-found freedom in this thrilling new pony-land. Alice tried to grab the rope, but just missed it as Tinks charged off to tell everyone she'd arrived and the party could begin.

Katy watched her squealing, heel-kicking progress with numb disbelief. Why did this sort of thing always happen to her? All the other ponies were perfectly behaved – at least they had been until Tinks had made her grand entry.

A pony being unloaded at the same time had broken

free now, and the two of them pranced around each other before setting off at speed to recruit new outlaws from the pens around the back, their lead ropes snaking perilously between their legs. Katy and Alice hurried after the brown backsides but, by the time they caught up, Tinks and her partner in crime had been guided into individual pens by some capable Exmoor pony people – including Mr Wright, the Secretary of the Exmoor Pony Society, and Mrs Soames.

"Ha! Katy, my dear! I should have guessed this little troublemaker was something to do with you!" Mrs Soames said jovially. "Cracking filly, mind."

Katy felt her face blushing with a mixture of embarrassment and pride. Mrs Soames was an authority on Exmoors and didn't hand out compliments about other people's ponies lightly. "Yes, sorry, thank you," she said, feeling incredibly foolish.

"Granfer here?" Mrs Soames asked. Just then, a whinny with the intensity of a foghorn came from the direction of the trailer park.

Tinks didn't appear to notice – she was too busy making friends with the ponies on either side of her – but Katy recognised it straightaway. "Oh, I almost forgot! Granfer's with Trifle, and she's still in the trailer!"

Trifle soon calmed down once she'd been put in a pen next to Tinks. Gradually the pens filled up with ponies and the passageways became crowded with people looking at them and talking to their owners.

Some of the ponies were quite timid and stood at the back of their pens where nobody could touch them. Not Tinks! She couldn't get enough attention, and poked her head sideways though the bars in an attempt to get closer to her adoring public. Katy was chatting to a potential customer from Scotland when out of the corner of her eye she saw a mother with her little girl, who was wiggling her fingers playfully under the filly's mouth. Tinks had become much better about not nipping people, but that was just asking for trouble.

"Excuse me, but I wouldn't do that if I were you," Katy said. "She's only young, and she could bite."

The mother gave Katy a black look and shepherded her child away. "Not that one, darling. It's nasty and vicious," she said in a loud voice. When Katy turned round again, the man from Scotland had gone.

Mrs Cunningham, whose ponies were in the pen opposite, rolled her eyes. "Some people! I do despair!"

Katy smiled shyly. Mary Cunningham was a well-respected moorland breeder who regularly won at shows. She was no-nonsense and opinionated. Even so, Katy would always be grateful to her because she'd made the decision to pass Trifle at her crucial second inspection.

"I've just been talking to your grandfather," Mrs

Cunningham said. "Hear you've had a spot of bother with your ponies on the moor. Seems you're not the only one."

"Oh?"

"Several people have been having problems this summer – gates left open, livestock where they shouldn't be, that sort of thing."

"Our ponies must have been frightened by something," Katy said. "It looks as if they broke the fence down and scrambled over the hedge. They've never done that before. A colt foal – Trifle's brother – was badly injured, too."

Mrs Cunningham became animated as she warmed to the subject. "Chased by a dog, or dogs, I expect. Trouble is, the general public hasn't got a clue about animals and the countryside, *not – a – clue*. People think they can do whatever they like on moorland, including allowing 'darling Fido' to run after anything that moves. They don't realise the National Park doesn't actually belong to them . . . My neighbour had her new trailer stolen the other day, and sheep have been taken from around South Molton, apparently. I don't know what the world's coming to, I really don't . . ." She began to catalogue other crimes she'd heard about, and what the police had or hadn't done about them. Katy looked for Alice, hoping she'd come and rescue her, but she was chatting to some old Pony

Club friends. Luckily James and Olivia turned up, though, so Katy excused herself.

James obviously felt uncomfortable among so many people.

"Would you like to brush Trifle?" Katy asked.

He nodded vigorously, so she handed him his favourite soft brush and they went into the pen together. Just to be on the safe side, with so many people and ponies everywhere, Katy put Trifle's head collar on her and tied her up.

James set to work, as careful and methodical as ever.

"Can we stroke your pony?" Two little girls wearing sundresses and sandals stood outside Trifle's pen, gazing longingly at her.

"If your parents don't mind," Katy agreed.

Katy stood back as James showed them the best way to introduce themselves to Trifle, by letting her see and smell them, and how to stay in her line of vision so they didn't alarm her. Then, as they were so good with her, he taught them how to groom her gently – not so gently that it tickled like a fly, but not hard enough to be uncomfortable either. He explained it all so calmly and confidently that Katy couldn't help smiling to herself. Only a few months ago she'd taught him the very same thing.

Soon a crowd had gathered around to watch, including a newspaper reporter who was jotting down information about each pony and its herd.

Katy told him how she'd fallen in love with Trifle the day she'd seen her struggling for survival as a newborn foal on the Common, and how she'd been determined to own her one day – so determined that she'd secretly bought her. She also touched on some of the highlights of their life together at Barton Farm, including how she'd saved Granfer after his quad bike accident on the moor, the Pure Gold Pets award and, of course, the birth of Tinks. Finally, she told him how James had moved into the farmhouse next door, how he and Trifle had developed an amazing relationship and how she'd made his life better in so many ways. He'd helped Trifle, too, by having her on loan because Katy had become too tall to ride her much.

"She's certainly a credit to you. A great ambassador for the breed as well as the Barton herd," the reporter said.

Katy was very glad he hadn't been around when she'd unloaded Tinks – or, to be precise, when Tinks had unloaded herself.

By the time the two little girls had finished grooming Trifle she shone so brightly you had to squint to look at her. Even her hooves had been polished. Eventually their parents managed to prise them away with the promise of ice cream, James decided he wanted to go home and Alice came back from seeing her friends.

Katy felt hot and thirsty. She was just about to go

and buy an ice cream and cold drink with Alice when Mrs Soames came hobbling up to them. Katy was sure she'd been all right earlier, but didn't like to ask.

"All set for your camping trip?" she asked.

"Sort of," Katy said. "I mean, we're really looking forward to it, but I'm afraid things haven't exactly gone to plan recently, what with Jacko losing a shoe and having an injured foal to look after, so we haven't done much in the way of getting ready yet."

"If it would help, you can always sleep in proper beds in the farmhouse. I don't mind one jot. That way you won't have to worry about camping gear."

Katy and Alice looked at each other, grinned and thanked her but said they'd like to camp because it would be more fun to be outside with their horses.

"Can't say I blame you," Mrs Soames replied. "If I were a few years younger I'd join you like a shot. Nothing I used to like better than travelling the moor with my pony and sleeping under the stars. Getting old's a frightful bore, you know. Avoid it like the plague." She winced and leaned against Tinks' pen.

"Are you okay, Mrs Soames?" Alice asked.

"Been better," she muttered. "Just tripped over one of those ridiculous extending leads with a terrier at the end of it. Done something to my leg. Couldn't be worse timing, with Exford in a couple of days. You're going, I take it?"

"Just for the afternoon," Alice replied. "Mum didn't want to close the stables for the whole day. I think we're planning on arriving around lunchtime. I'm riding Max in the inter-hunt relay and my stepfather, Dean, is doing a horse agility demonstration with him."

Tinks came up and nuzzled Mrs Soames' arm.

She stroked her in return and said, "Pity you aren't a colt foal, or I'd snap you up as a stallion-in-waiting. I'd love to introduce Tormentil's bloodlines into my herd. She's what I call a good old-fashioned sort. Hard to find nowadays. I presume you're showing this filly and her mum at Exford on Wednesday, Katy?"

"I'm afraid not," she replied. "Tinks was born in December and, as you know, ponies have to be born after the first of January this year to qualify as foals, so she sort of falls between the gaps. If I'd got around to weaning her in time, I could have shown her in the yearling class and Trifle in a couple of classes as well, I suppose, but I missed the deadline for entries." All of a sudden Katy felt sad she hadn't got her act together. Going to Exford with nothing to show wasn't nearly as much fun as taking part.

"You'll be going anyway, I take it?"

"Yes, with Granfer."

"Excellent! I was planning to show Kestrel, my stallion. Shan't be able to now – not with a gammy knee. You can do it instead."

Katy stared at her, wondering whether she'd heard correctly. She had no idea how to show a stallion. Come to think of it, she didn't even know the stallion she'd be showing! What a crazy idea.

Mrs Soames beamed at her. "Come and meet him. He's over here, away from the mares and foals." She hobbled off down the line of pens, with Katy and Alice following. "I thought it would be good experience for him to come today. Been running with the herd on the moor until three days ago."

"So he hasn't done any showing?" Alice posed the question Katy didn't dare ask.

"Not since he was a youngster," Mrs Soames replied over her shoulder. "He'll be fine, though."

Like I thought Tinks would be fine, Katy said to herself.

But as soon as she saw Kestrel she was smitten. There was something about him that set him apart. Perhaps it was his fathomless amber eyes, which pierced Katy like lasers, or his cool self-confidence. His beautiful head had unusually chiselled features for an Exmoor stallion, but that made him even more charismatic.

He politely brushed the back of her outstretched hand with his muzzle in greeting, like a gallant gentleman.

She knew there and then she couldn't turn down this opportunity. It would be an honour to show him at Exford.

80

# 8

# A Stallion to Show

O f all the summer shows, Exford was Katy's favourite. In many ways it was more like a party than a show because almost everyone on Exmoor went.

Walking around the showground with Granfer was almost impossible, even though it was early when they arrived. As soon as he wound up a conversation with one lot of friends, he bumped into some more and started all over again.

In the end Katy left him talking and went to the competitors' car park to see if Kestrel had arrived.

She found Mrs Soames' trailer hiding behind a large horse lorry at the end of a line of vehicles. The horses in the lorry were having bandages, travel boots and tail guards removed, tails brushed, plaits sewn, coats polished and hooves oiled.

Mrs Soames led Kestrel down the ramp. He looked magnificent just as he was, glistening in the sunlight, wearing only a head collar . . . And there were those eyes again, half hidden by his luxurious forelock, looking straight into her.

"Here you are. All yours," Mrs Soames said, handing Katy his lead rope.

I wish, Katy thought.

Mrs Soames looked at her watch. "We've got about forty minutes. Lead him around. Get to know each other. Give him a brush, if you like; there's a grooming kit on the passenger seat. I'll go and get your number from the Secretary's tent. The walk will do me good."

"Thanks," Katy said, letting Kestrel sniff her hand before taking hold of the lead rope. "Oh, how's your knee?"

"Grumbling, but I refuse to listen," Mrs Soames replied.

Left alone with the awe-inspiring stallion, Katy felt ridiculously awkward and unsure of what to do. She decided to tie him to the trailer and groom him first –

not because he needed it, but because it was a good way of getting to know any horse.

Although Mrs Soames appeared eccentric, she was well organised. Her grooming kit was fairly basic but it was clean and of the best quality. Katy chose a soft leather-backed body brush and set to work, noticing straight away that Kestrel smelled of horse rather than shampoo. Mrs Soames was undoubtedly old-school, like Granfer, and cleaned ponies the hard way: by brushing rather than washing them.

It was amazing how different Kestrel was from Trifle or Tinks, apart from typical stallion traits like a thick neck and lots of hair. His body was well-muscled and athletic. He'd spent the summer on open moorland, taking lots of exercise and eating rough grasses, whereas they'd been pampered at home.

Katy started by grooming safe areas like his mane, withers and back, then moved to his tummy and his face. He stood patiently, not obviously enjoying it but not objecting either. She began to relax with him, and almost forgot she wasn't grooming one of her own ponies as she bent over to brush his front leg.

*Bam!* With lightning speed he lifted his leg up, hitting the side of the trailer with his hoof.

Katy leapt back in shock.

A man's head appeared out of the cab of the horse lorry next door. "You okay?"

"Er, yes, thanks," she replied shakily.

"What happened?" the man asked.

"I don't really know. I was brushing his leg, but I don't think he liked it for some reason. He's been fine until now."

"Stallion, is he?"

"Yes."

"Know him well?"

"No, not really. I mean today's the first time I've groomed him or anything."

"There's your answer, then. Most stallions hate having their legs touched. It's a survival thing. Legs are really important. If a horse injures one it can mean death."

Katy instantly thought of Simba.

"That's why stallions go for each other's legs when they're fighting, to cause maximum damage. It's also why horses in general, and stallions in particular, aren't happy about people they don't trust touching their legs."

It all made perfect sense to Katy, even though it was upsetting to think Kestrel didn't trust her. Anxiously, she inspected Kestrel's foreleg from a safe distance, and was glad she couldn't see any cuts or swelling. She decided not to take him for a walk. Instead she brushed his tail strand by strand, to look as if she was doing something useful.

Eventually Mrs Soames came back, carrying Katy's competitor number. "All set? You'll be on in about ten minutes."

Katy felt a surge of panic. She hadn't even led Kestrel yet, but she didn't want to admit that.

"I'll put his bridle on while you get ready," Mrs Soames said.

With growing apprehension Katy put on her jacket, wiped the dust off her ankle boots and tied her number around her waist.

Kestrel looked even more magnificent now he was wearing his brown show bridle with brass fittings.

Mrs Soames handed Katy the leather lead rein, which attached to the rings on each side of his bit with a smart brass chain that jangled when Kestrel shook his head. "He does that if you hold him too tight," Mrs Soames said. "Give him room to move freely and keep your hands nice and soft, like you would if you were riding him."

Katy frowned, cross with herself. She was so nervous that she'd forgotten all the things she'd learned in horse agility about leading horses correctly.

"Don't look so worried!" Mrs Soames said. "He'll be fine."

Katy took a deep breath and tried to concentrate on the "candle trick" Dean had taught her – picturing a candle inside herself and being in control of the flame.

She took her imaginary flame right down low and instantly felt calmer. Kestrel stopped fidgeting, too.

"All set?" asked Mrs Soames.

"Think so."

"Off we go, then."

Kestrel bubbled with energy, but his manners were impeccable. He kept pace with Katy, never pulled, pricked his ears and stepped out beautifully. It was hard to imagine he'd been running with his herd on the moor until a week ago. His early training must have been really thorough.

Heads turned in admiration as they made their way to the collecting ring. We'll definitely be in with a chance, Katy thought, and smiled to herself. Perhaps she was more competitive than she liked to admit.

There were only four other stallions in the class. Unfortunately they all looked fabulous, though. Katy knew at least one of them had been to the Horse of the Year Show. Kestrel was smaller and slimmer than the others. Would that count against him?

It wasn't even eleven o'clock yet, and already the sun was so hot it made wearing a tweed jacket almost unbearable, but she kept smiling as they paraded in front of the judge. The ground underfoot was like concrete and the grass had a sickly, scorched look. There hadn't been any rain for ages.

The steward asked them to halt when they got to one

corner, and then they had to trot round the ring in turn – rather like having to circle to the end of the ride in a riding lesson. After that, their numbers were called out for the preliminary line-up.

Katy and Kestrel were fourth.

At least it isn't fifth, she said to herself, stroking his magnificent neck. How could the judge not think he was the best? He definitely had the best manners. The one in second position looked grumpy and the third one kept trying to nip his handler.

The individual inspections and shows followed, after which they all had to walk around in a circle again while the judge made his final decision.

Fifth.

Katy did her best to hide her disappointment.

"Well done, and thank you so much. Some stiff opposition there," Mrs Soames said when Katy joined her and Granfer by the ringside.

"Wrong judge for him, that's the top and bottom of it," Granfer said. On several occasions he'd told Katy that different judges liked certain types of Exmoor, and it was a waste of time entering a competition if you knew the judge wouldn't like your pony.

Katy looked fondly at Kestrel as he stood by her side, calmly interested in the bustling showground. Why hadn't the judge been able to see he was easily the best? Showing was more like a lottery than a fair contest. Surely there had to be agreement on what everyone was looking for, or there was no point.

"Yes, jolly unfortunate," Mrs Soames said. "I must admit my main reason for bringing Kestrel today was to get him seen by as many people as possible in the hope someone will take him on. His daughters will be coming into the herd next year, so I can't keep him however much I'd love to. I've put an advertisement up in the Secretary's tent, but I doubt whether anyone will be interested now. People set great store by a red rosette."

Katy smoothed Kestrel's forelock so it didn't flop into his eyes, and he gently bent his head round, as if thanking her. You are utterly gorgeous, she thought. Exactly the sort of stallion I'd love to run with the Barton herd next year. You'll probably be far too expensive, though. I'll need all my money to get Simba straight. She caught Granfer's eye, and imagined him saying, *"Strike while the iron's hot, maid."*

"Um, you know you said you wanted to sell Kestrel next year?"

"Oh, I'd never sell him!" Mrs Soames replied, dashing Katy's hopes. "He's such a sweetheart," she went on. "I bought him from Mary, fresh off the moor, and he was the easiest colt I've ever handled. He passes his temperament on to his foals, too. No, I won't ever sell him, but I will be looking for a loan home next year, for a couple of seasons at least." A slow smile spread across her weatherworn face. "You interested?"

"Yes, very," Katy replied.

"Excellent!" Mrs Soames gave Kestrel's neck a gentle pat. "He'll love it on the Common with those wonderful mares of yours. It'll be a good match genetics-wise, too. There's a rare bloodline on his sire's side, so we'll be doing our bit for the breed. I couldn't be happier."

"Neither could I," Katy said, finding it hard to believe what she'd just arranged.

Granfer beamed at her. "That's my girl. You're a good judge of horseflesh, and no mistake."

Katy smiled back. His approval was better than winning first prize in the show ring. "Shall I take Kestrel back to the box and give him some water?" she asked.

"By all means, but don't let him roll or get hay in his mane," Mrs Soames replied. "He's qualified for the In Hand Moor Bred Championships – should be around twelve-thirty."

"But we came fifth out of five!" Katy hardly liked to remind her.

"Even so, he was the highest-placed Exmoor-bred pony in the class," Mrs Soames said.

"Robert's judging the Championships. He'll be

much better – got his head screwed on," Granfer said.

"Oh. Do you think we're in with a chance?" Katy asked.

"Maybe. We'll have to wait and see who you're up against," Mrs Soames replied.

As Katy led Kestrel into the ring for the second time that day, she heard the main ring commentator announcing Dean's horse agility demonstration with Max. Shows were often like that: hours of waiting followed by clashing events. She'd seen Dean doing horse agility many times, but never ceased to be amazed by what he'd achieved with Max. Anyway, she should be concentrating on Kestrel and this Championship competition rather than what was going on elsewhere. With eight beautiful prizewinning ponies in the class, Kestrel didn't stand a chance of winning, but she'd rather not come last again. Mrs Soames had been noble in defeat, but she was fiercely competitive and Katy knew it had upset her.

Glancing into the centre of the ring, she was sure she recognised the tall, thick-set man judging the Moor Bred Championship. He looked more like a heavy hunter judge than a pony judge. Where had she met him before?

To her astonishment, they were pulled in third for the preliminary line-up. Perhaps they'd been asked in at random – that happened sometimes.

It wasn't until the judge was inspecting Kestrel that Katy realised where she'd seen him before: he'd awarded Trifle the Mountain and Moorland Championship at Dunster Show! She wondered whether he recognised her. If he did, he didn't let on.

Kestrel behaved perfectly during his individual show, echoing Katy's moves exactly and stepping out impressively. Mrs Cunningham, standing at the head of the line-up with her prizewinning mare, grinned at them as they went past. Her face looked totally different when she smiled.

The judge took a long time over each pony, giving the same amount of attention to each one. As soon as he'd seen all the ponies, though, he made his decision quickly. He placed Mrs Cunningham's mare first, Kestrel second, a young gelding third and a mare and foal fourth.

"In first place, and winner of the Moorland Cup, Mrs Mary Cunningham's veteran mare, Fernleigh Goldfinch," the commentator said. "Second place, Mrs Eileen Soames' stallion, Fernleigh Kestrel, bred by Mrs Cunningham, out of Goldfinch . . ."

Katy didn't hear the names of the other ponies. So that was Kestrel's mum! Looking at the mare, she could see the likeness. She exchanged smiles with Mrs Cunningham and the other competitors, feeling a wonderful sense of belonging. She wasn't a Pony Club kid any more; she was an Exmoor pony breeder, showing the stallion who, all being well, would sire some wonderful foals for her one day.

When Katy and Kestrel left the arena, Mrs Soames, Granfer, Alice, Dean and Melanie came up to congratulate them. The horse agility demonstration had finished just in time for the final line-up.

Another moorland breeder joined them. "Mr Wright tells me you're looking for a home for your stallion next year," she said to Mrs Soames. "I'd love to have him."

"Thanks so much, but I'm afraid he's already spoken for," Mrs Soames replied. "He's going to the Barton herd."

The lady looked disappointed and walked away.

"See what I mean, Katy? Apart from you, nobody was interested in him before the Championships, but she's the third person to ask me about him since he did well," Mrs Soames said.

Granfer patted Katy's arm. "Pays to strike while the iron's hot, see?" He pulled his wallet out of his trouser pocket. "Talking of being hot, who'd like an ice cream? I've been watching that van next to the stags' horns for ages, hoping the queue would get shorter, but it never does."

Needless to say, they all wanted one. Alice and Katy went to help Granfer carry them while Mrs Soames held Kestrel and chatted to his admirers.

The queue was long and slow-moving, so the girls had plenty of time to look at the stags' horns laid out on trestle tables for the various competitions: pairs of horns, single horns and unusual-looking horns. There were so many it was difficult to concentrate on just one. Katy and Alice agreed judging them would be an awful job, especially when people took such a keen interest in this part of the show. Everyone had an opinion, including Granfer. He told the girls exactly which ones should win, and why.

"I can't help thinking it's wrong to shoot a stag just to get its antlers," Alice said. She never called antlers "horns" like the locals.

"Couldn't agree more," Granfer said. "These aren't from stags that have been killed, though. They're found."

"Oh, like the antlers we sometimes find on the ground? The ones that are shed each spring?"

"The very same."

"But it must be impossible to find a pair," Alice said.

"Tricky, but not impossible. You've got to know where to look – racks in the hedges, for instance. Often the jolt of landing will be enough for a stag to cast one. It's a tremendous hobby hereabouts. I used to be keen when I was younger. Too many people do it nowadays. Too many stags are getting poached, as well. They take the best heads, leaving the second-rate ones to breed. 'Tis a shame, really."

"Next, please!" called the harassed ice-cream seller.

"Six large vanilla ices in those chocolate waffle cone doodahs with chocolate flakes in them, if you please." Granfer winked at the girls. "Pour boldly or not at all."

Katy took a cone in each hand. "Thanks, Granfer. That's definitely one of your best sayings!"

# 9

# The Beach Barbecue

A few days after Exford Show, the heatwave broke in spectacular fashion, with thunderstorms and torrential rain. Sharon and Adam came over to see Simba in the afternoon.

"I'm so glad the horses at the yard are in their stables," Sharon said as they stood in the sheep shed listening to hail hurtling down on the roof and thunder rumbling all around.

"And *I'm* glad because Simba's doing well," Katy said.

Adam crouched down to inspect Simba's wound.

"Better than I dared hope. No more pus, no smell – everything's healing nicely, thanks to your expert nursing. If you like, you could apply a thin layer of honey under the dressing strip to keep everything moist and healthy. It shouldn't be long before a pink halo appears around the edge of this granulation tissue. That'll be the new skin forming from the outside." He smiled up at her. "It can't have been easy, but your hard work's paying off."

"Catching him and holding him steady has been the hardest part," Katy said. "Dad and Tom have done that for me. They were the only people strong enough to begin with. It's better now I can get a head collar on him, though. Alice helped me last night, and he was fine. Oh, and the other good news is Dad says he doesn't mind looking after him while Alice and I go away for a couple of nights, so we can still go on our riding holiday."

"That's great." Adam stood up. "I must admit I hadn't really thought about how difficult it would be to treat a completely wild foal. All my training's been with domesticated horses. In fact, I'd had very little experience of horses and ponies until I met Sharon."

"He's a quick learner. Had to be," she said.

Katy gently scratched Simba's short mane. He no longer flinched away when she touched him. "This one's a quick learner, too. Trifle's helped a lot. I think she must send out comforting vibes that show him there's nothing to worry about."

"Like now," Sharon said.

They all looked at Trifle, who was eating hay, apparently deaf to the extreme weather outside.

"As long as she's got food, she's okay," Katy said.

There was a moment's silence as they all stood mesmerised by the comforting sound of steady munching.

"Oh, I know what I wanted to ask you," Katy said. "Are you going to the Stonyford beach barbecue? I do hope so!" Alice had told her they'd been invited. As the day drew closer she'd begun to dread it, but if Sharon and Adam were there it wouldn't be so bad. Perhaps they'd be able to go for a walk along the beach instead of swimming.

"Sadly, no," Sharon answered. "I'm taking a couple of horses to a show on Saturday."

Katy remembered Alice had said the friends from Pony Club she'd invited couldn't go to the party because they were going to a horse show. At this rate she'd hardly know anyone.

"And I'm working all weekend," Adam said. "Are you sure they're going ahead with it? The weather forecast's appalling."

"You mean they might cancel?"

Adam climbed over the side of Simba's pen. "Don't

ask me. But my idea of a good time definitely isn't a beach barbecue in the pouring rain."

I couldn't agree more, Katy thought.

After that she kept a close watch on the weather forecast. It looked hopeful: another low pressure system out in the Atlantic was gathering momentum as it headed for the west coast of Britain. High winds and heavy rain were inevitable. Katy had never longed so fervently for bad weather.

U nfortunately Melanie wasn't the sort of person who was put off by a bit of rain. The weekend had been planned for ages, and they had lots of guests staying, so it wouldn't have been easy to call the whole thing off. Also, it turned out the weather forecasters had got things slightly wrong: the storm that was supposed to sweep across the south-west on Saturday blew through on Friday night, leaving an overcast but dry day and rough seas in its wake.

"Fab surfing conditions!" Alice declared when she greeted Katy, Mum and Dad on the grey, windy beach. She looked stunning in her wetsuit, with her long blonde hair and deeply tanned face.

Most of the people Katy's age were wearing wetsuits, by the looks of it. Some were in the water already, swimming or surfing. She didn't have a wetsuit or a surfboard, just a boring plain blue swimming costume underneath her jeans and sweatshirt.

"Come and meet everyone!" Alice said, taking Katy's hand and running down to the shore. Katy ran with her, feeling embarrassed and out of place.

Sophie, Pete, Livi, Kate, Cameron, Fi, Tim, Jonathan, Laura, Harry, Natasha, Tory, Louisa . . . Alice's friends from school and her old home in Surrey were sophisticated and self-confident. They greeted Katy enthusiastically, but she felt so shy that she hardly said a word.

"Um, how about a drink?" Alice said. "It's all up there." She pointed to a large tent strategically placed above the high tide mark at the base of the sand dunes.

"Good idea," Katy said.

Alice hesitated.

"Don't worry, you carry on surfing," Katy insisted.

"Are you sure?"

"Quite sure."

Alice gave her a hug. "Come on down when you're ready. You can borrow my surfboard."

"I can't surf."

"Never mind. I'll teach you. It'll be fun!"

"Er, okay, perhaps later." Why was it so difficult to tell Alice she was scared of the sea?

The tent was full of adults drinking wine out of plastic cups, trying to get the portable barbecues going and making upbeat remarks like, "At least it isn't raining."

Katy sipped her cup of Coke as slowly as she could and latched on to Dad, who was talking to a farmer from Surrey. Actually, they were shouting rather than talking. It was hard to be heard above the noise of the wind, the flapping tent and everyone talking louder and louder.

If only James had come! They could have kept each other company – gone for a walk along the beach or something. Olivia had taken him to see his grandparents, and Katy had promised to look after Trifle while they were away. She wished she were at home with the ponies right this minute.

It was tempting to stick with Dad, but she was the only teenager in the tent and she didn't want to look like Katy-no-mates. Everyone else of her age was down by the sea. She'd have to go and join them.

Summoning all her courage, she set off towards the foaming, crashing waves and the dark shapes frolicking around in them like seals. How wonderful to be able to think of the sea as a thrilling playground! She felt sick with apprehension, yet she kept going, heading for a group who were making a massive sandcastle. Perhaps she could avoid surfing by helping them.

Desperation made her bold. "Hi, I'm Katy," she said cheerfully.

Several of them looked up. "Yes, we met earlier. I'm Laura," said a tall, slim redhead.

"Can I help with your sandcastle?"

"You'll have to ask the Works Supervisor," Laura said, pointing towards a suntanned, fair-haired boy wearing Bermuda shorts. "Hey, Tim! Got a job for Katy?"

"It would be great if we could have more sand for the fortifications at the front here. You can get it from the moat, or start another ditch in front if you like," he said.

"No problem." Katy set to work. Having helped out at Barton Farm all her life, she was pretty good at shovelling and carrying. The practical farmer in her thought that building something with military precision when it would be destroyed almost instantly was a strange way to waste energy, but she was glad to do anything that didn't involve swimming in the sea.

It soon became apparent that the castle-construction party members all knew each other well. Katy was definitely the odd one out, so she was relieved when several others joined in, including Alice.

They did their best to include her, but Katy shrank away from the clever banter and in-jokes of Alice and her friends. She hadn't felt so lacking in confidence since she'd been at primary school. She'd never felt easy with the in-crowd, whether at school, Pony Club or anywhere else. There was no doubt about it: she definitely preferred one-to-one friendships. "I'll go and see if I can find some shells to decorate the sides with," she said, picking up a bucket.

Alice leapt nimbly from the centre of the castle where she'd been putting the finishing touches on a turret. "I'll come too."

They wandered along the shoreline in silence, looking for shells in the dull, damp sand. Alice at the seaside in a wetsuit was like a stranger.

"Hard to believe it's summer," Katy said.

"Yes, isn't it? Are you okay, Katy?"

"Yes, fine."

"Really?"

Katy hoped her smile was convincing. "Yes, really."

Eventually they decided to turn back, and came face to face with two men taking a couple of dogs for a walk. It took a moment for Katy to recognise the younger, smaller man. She'd only ever seen him in a delivery van before.

"Hi, Dave."

He didn't seem at all pleased to see her. "Oh, hi," he replied. Definitely not his usual talkative self.

"I like your dogs." She didn't particularly, but felt she had to say something. They were big, muscular, light brown and rather scary-looking, and the largest one was wearing a muzzle.

"Oh, they're not mine," Dave said. "They belong to Roddy."

Roddy scowled at Dave. Maybe he wanted to get on, or he didn't like talking to people, or both.

"Oh, right. Er, bye then," Katy said, and they went their separate ways.

"Charming," Alice said in a half-whisper.

"Delightful," Katy agreed, and they grinned at each other.

"Hey, look at this." Katy pointed to the pawprints left by the dogs in some soft sand. "How amazing!"

"Pawprints," Alice remarked, clearly unimpressed.

"Yes, but look closely," Katy said. "The larger dog – the one with the muzzle – must have had some sort of accident because he's lopsided, see? There's a complete pad missing from the outside of one of his paws."

"You're observant. I'd never have noticed that."

Katy smiled. "James has taught me well. The point is, we both saw a pawprint like that on the Common, near where the ponies and deer broke into Moor Field when Simba got caught up in the fence. I bet that dog was chasing them!"

"Gosh, that's serious. Should we call the police?"

"I'd like to, but they can hardly arrest someone for taking their dogs for a walk. Stupidly, I didn't even take a photo of the pawprint on the Common, and Dad ran over it with the tractor before I could show it to him, so only James and I saw it."

"I suppose even if the police had seen it, or a photo, it wouldn't have proved anything."

"Perhaps not, but it may have helped if they've already got other evidence."

Alice pulled her phone from a neoprene holder. She took some photos of the men and dogs as they walked away, and some of the pawprints as well. "Just in case."

Katy stared after them. From a distance, the dogs looked rather like lions, she thought. Her gaze shifted to the incoming tide. "Hey, the sea's nearly reached the castle!"

"Let's run!" Alice set off like a gazelle. Katy followed as quickly as she could, the shells they'd picked up clattering around in her bucket.

Alice and her friends gathered in the centre of the castle, hugging each other, taking selfies and becoming more and more excited as the waves crept closer. "Come on, Katy, there's room for one more!" she called.

"Budge up, everyone," Tim said, and beckoned to Katy.

She clambered awkwardly over the ramparts, accidentally squishing a section with her foot. The whole thing would be demolished in a few minutes, but it still made her feel awful.

Tim put his arm around her shoulder and drew her

in for the group photo. Katy could feel herself blushing terribly – it would show in the photo for sure.

"Hang on! We need one with you in it, too, Laura," Alice said.

"I'll do it," Katy volunteered. She'd much rather take photos than be in them.

"Are you sure?"

"Sure I'm sure."

"Brilliant, thanks!" Alice handed her phone over.

Katy stumbled out of the castle again, alarmed to see a wave breaching the first trench. She'd have to hurry – those breakers were far too close for comfort. She positioned the phone and held it steady. "Say cheese."

"Cheese!" the friends shouted in unison.

Worried that she hadn't got everyone in, she stepped back a few paces. Water lapped around her feet, soaking the bottom of her jeans, but she had her back to the sea and was so intent on getting the perfect shot that she hardly noticed.

*Whooosh!*

Katy's feet were swept from under her as a wave hit her legs. For a desperate moment she tried to regain her balance, but it was hopeless. She fell into a chaos of surf and sand that pulled her backwards as it flowed towards the sea again.

*The phone! She'd dropped Alice's phone!* Through a blur of water, she spotted a white object skimming away from her, carried by the current. Desperate not to lose it, she lunged after it, throwing herself into the water. *Yes!* Her fingers curled round the precious phone just as another wave rushed in, filling her mouth with salty, gritty liquid. It made her gag, then cough convulsively. Terrified and gasping for breath, she crawled through the swirling water, gripping the phone as if her life depended on it. Her sodden jeans and sweatshirt felt heavy and constricting.

Suddenly lots of legs were splashing around her. People were shouting, lifting her to safety. She handed the phone to someone and caught a glimpse of the castle, a lumpy island now – its features erased, slowly but surely, by each destructive wave.

All that work, and in the end they'd missed the fun of watching it go, she thought, and then she threw up on the sand.

# 10

# Common Ground

A lice had invited Katy to Stonyford the next morning for a big lunch party with all the weekend guests, but she couldn't face it. She was too embarrassed about the beach fiasco. Whenever she thought about it – which was all the time – it made her cringe inside. If she'd disliked Alice's friends she wouldn't have cared so much about what they thought of her, but they'd all been really kind, despite the fact they must have thought she was a complete idiot.

After changing the dressing on Simba's leg and putting the ponies out in the paddock, she sat down on the woolsack and told Simba about what had happened. "I suppose the only good thing that's come out of this is I understand what you've been through a bit better," she said when she'd finished. "You must have been completely terrified to begin with. I expect you thought we wanted to kill you, like I felt the waves wanted to kill me yesterday. You've been unbelievably brave, little man." She smiled. "In fact, as James would say, you've faced your fears like Simba."

Recognising the sound of his name, he rested his head on the top of the pen and looked at her with his big, bright eyes.

It struck her that baby Exmoor ponies and baby red deer calves were remarkably similar – legs, eyes and swivelling ears, all alert and ready for action. She got up from the woolsack, went over to him and rubbed his neck. "Poor Simba," she whispered. "It must be awful to be ready for action yet not allowed to move. I'd love to give you a larger pen, so you can run around and play, but Adam says I mustn't. If you move too much it could make you lame for life." She sighed. "My stupid problems are nothing compared with what you're having to cope with, are they?" Her hand reached his withers, and she scratched them gently.

He leaned towards her, his muzzle quivering with enjoyment.

Seeing him like that, Katy couldn't help feeling

happy. "Okay, funny face," she said eventually. "I'll get some more grass for you, as a special treat, and then I'm going to take Jacko for a ride while the weather's okay. They're forecasting rain for this afternoon. I bet you've almost forgotten what rain is, haven't you?"

Jacko was his usual cheerful self, glad to be out and eager to please. It was rare to find a pony so comfortable with life that it made no difference to him whether he was going away from home or towards it, nor whether he had others for company. The more Katy got to know horses, the more she realised how lucky she was. Going for a ride on Jacko was always a pleasure. She never had to think twice; she just saddled up and went in whatever direction she fancied, which was invariably to the wide-open spaces of the Common.

I feel at home here, she thought. Every animal has a natural habitat, and this is mine. Embarrassing memories melted away as Jacko cantered over the purple-tinged moorland. In a few days the heather would be in full bloom and Katy would be on holiday with Alice. Their friendship was always at its strongest when they were riding alone together on Exmoor. The fact that Alice and Katy had different friends nowadays, or that Alice was aiming for A grades in her exams whereas Katy would be pleased if she passed, or that Alice had been on holiday to seven different countries but Katy had never been abroad, didn't matter at all when they were riding with each other. This would be their first holiday without any grown-ups telling them where to go and what to do; just Katy, Jacko, Alice and Max. What an adventure!

Katy spent a lot of time with her ponies during the next couple of days, grooming Simba and going for long rides on Jacko, as well as doing some horse agility with Jacko, Trifle and Tinks.

It didn't take her long to realise that although Simba looked to Trifle for reassurance, Tinks had become his special friend. They couldn't seem to get enough of each other's company. She often found them touching muzzles through the pens or just resting with their heads as close as possible.

It was Alice who spotted the great advantage of this when she visited the farm on Wednesday to plan their holiday. "Why don't you leave Simba and Tinks together in adjoining pens while we take Trifle and Jacko out for a ride?" she asked. "That way, you can gently start the weaning process."

"Brilliant idea," Katy said, glad of a reason to do something. They'd both avoided mentioning the beach party so far, and it was becoming awkward. "I'll just go and see if someone can keep an eye on Tinks and Simba while we're away."

As luck would have it, Dad said he didn't mind spending an hour or two in the barn as there were some gates that needed mending.

Katy had to ride Trifle bareback because her legs were too long for the saddle now. In fact, her legs weren't very far off the ground. It felt strange to be on an Exmoor pony again, like going back in time . . . Short neck with a bushy mane cascading over both sides, black-tipped ears always pointing forwards, a trot like a sewing machine and – oh dear – a lot of Trifle whinnies! She'd always put her heart and soul into whinnying, but now she had every reason to, with her foal left behind in the shed. Her whole body shook with the effort.

"This is hopeless. James will never be able to cope with the noise," Katy said.

"Compared with some of the horses Mum's weaned over the years, she's being incredibly good," Alice replied. "I mean, she's not doing anything naughty like napping and galloping for home, is she?" She grinned. "Rome wasn't built in a day, you know."

Katy laughed, the memories of training a much younger Trifle at Stonyford flooding back. "The *Rome wasn't built in a day* method of pony taming! Also known as the *I haven't a clue what I'm doing but we'll get there in the end* method. That seems so long ago, doesn't it?"

"Sort of, yet in a way it seems like yesterday." They'd reached the gate onto the Common. "Go on or turn back?" Alice asked.

"I don't know. I'm worried I might be too heavy for her."

"Nonsense!" Alice replied. "Your legs are so long that you could do with a set of roller skates, but you're not too heavy. She hasn't even broken out in a sweat, has she?"

"Let's go on, then. It might help take her mind off things."

Katy was right. As soon as Trifle was on the open moorland she developed a purposeful spring in her step.

"This is your natural habitat too, isn't it?" she said to Trifle, smoothing her mane.

"What?"

"Sorry, I was talking to Trifle," Katy said. "Being on the beach the other day, and then coming up here afterwards, got me thinking about whether we all have a natural habitat where we feel happy and at home. For me it's up here, and I think it's the same for Trifle as well." There – she'd broached the subject of the beach without really meaning to.

"That's an interesting idea. I wonder where mine is? Probably the beach. I must admit I've always found moorland a bit scary, especially the parts I don't know.

It's got better now I've learned which plants to look out for, but I'm a real wuss when it comes to boggy ground."

Katy smiled. "Just like I'm a wuss about the sea. I've been scared of swimming ever since a lifeguard had to save me when I was eight."

"I had no idea! You never said. Oh, and that wave crashing over you when you rescued my phone! You must have been petrified. I'm so sorry."

"It wasn't your fault. I just felt sort of like a fish out of water – except I'd rather be out of water, of course."

"Poor you. I didn't realise."

"I hope your friends didn't think I was totally weird."

"Not at all." Alice grinned. "In fact, I got the impression Tim liked you, *a lot*. He couldn't get over how much sand you managed to carry. You should keep in touch. He's lovely, and his family are super-rich. His dad owns a huge building firm in Surrey."

Katy laughed. "That explains why he was so good at organising the building work. There's a lot of difference between liking someone for their sand-hauling skills and liking them as in fancying them, you know."

Alice giggled. "Well, you definitely made an impression on him, and it's about time you thought about somebody other than Greg."

"Why?" Katy asked. Just the mention of his name made her cheeks flush.

"Because," Alice paused, "because he's working on a farm miles away, you hardly ever see him and he's much older than you, for starters. Oh, and you've never been anything other than good friends."

It was true, Katy had to admit, but she couldn't help hoping one day, when she was older, things would be different. "Did I tell you? He's coming back to Exmoor for Christmas," she said in reply.

"Oh, Katy! You're impossible!" Alice exclaimed.

"What about you? Didn't I see you and Jonathan with your arms around each other when everyone was in the castle?"

Now it was Alice's turn to blush. "The waves were even better as the tide came in after lunch, and he taught me how to surf properly. He's brilliant at it," she said. *"And* he's a brilliant rider. In fact, he's pretty well perfect . . ."

She talked about Jonathan for a while and then the conversation turned to horses, as it always did sooner or later.

"It's ages since I've ridden Jacko. I'd forgotten how wonderful he is," she said. "Horses that are advertised as fun usually aren't safe, and the ones that are safe are usually dead boring, but he really *is* fun and safe at the same time."

"Yes, I'm so lucky. I can't think why your mum wanted to sell him," Katy replied.

"I can. He was too good for Stonyford. He'd have been ruined by lots of different people riding him the whole time."

"Max seems to have survived."

"Ah, only a chosen few are allowed to ride him – even fewer now Dean's doing lots of horse agility. It's made him so obedient that most people can't cope."

"It's the same when normal people try to ride top dressage horses, isn't it?" Katy said. "They can't do a thing with them because they respond to the slightest cue, like a change in breathing."

"Reminds me of Viking. He was definitely hyper-sensitive. It's exhausting riding a horse like that. You have to concentrate the whole time. Give me Jacko any day." She reached forward and ran her hand down his mane. "He's a lovely colour, isn't he? I've always liked liver chestnut horses." She grinned. "Or chocolate, as you prefer to call it."

"Yes, how can such a beautiful colour have such an unattractive name – *liver* chestnut? Another one is dun. It's such a great colour but it sounds like dung."

"The Americans call it buckskin, which is much nicer. And light red chestnuts are sorrel. I love that . . ."

Before they knew it, they were back at the gate into Moor Field. Trifle automatically stood by the latch, pivoted around with the grace of a ballroom dancer and was as still as a statue while Katy leaned almost to the point of no return to shut it again. "Good girl! Have you noticed how settled she's become?" she said.

"Yes, soon James will be riding her out, no problem."

"I hope Tinks has been okay."

"Only one way to find out," Alice said.

Everything seemed quiet as they approached the barn – no hammering, sawing or power tools. Katy looked at her watch. They'd been far longer than they'd meant to be; had Dad given up babysitting?

As they reached the door, though, they heard Dad's voice. The girls looked at one another in surprise.

He was sitting on the woolsack, reading his *Farmers Weekly* magazine out loud to the ponies: "At Sedgemoor Market an entry of seventy-six prime cattle saw a flying trade, with steers averaging . . ."

Simba was nearly asleep on his feet, and Tinks was actually lying down.

"He's bored them into submission with the Market Report," Katy whispered, and both girls burst into giggles.

Dad looked up, slightly embarrassed. "Well, after I'd mended the gates I had to do something to pass the time, so I took Alice's advice and read these youngsters a bedtime story. Worked a treat, didn't it?"

The spell of being read to had been broken. Tinks got up and whinnied to her mum, and Trifle gave a dutiful whinny back. Simba whinnied to everyone.

Dad got up and stretched. "Next time I'm down here foal-sitting, I'll bring my sketch book. The colours of an Exmoor pony's head are very complex and attractive, aren't they? I don't know why I never noticed before. I might try to paint a portrait of Simba."

Katy had to stop her mouth from dropping open in surprise. Dad had painted most of the things on the farm – his farm animal portraits were particularly popular with the bed and breakfast guests – but until now he'd never attempted to paint an Exmoor pony. Granfer had made him ride Exmoors when he was a boy, and after several bad falls he'd become frightened of them.

It looked like Simba might be winning him round.

# 11

# The Big Adventure

Alice was right. Within a couple of days James was riding Trifle alongside Jacko on the leading rein, no problem. His confidence grew with every outing, and Trifle seemed to love her new job as a leading-rein pony. Katy was amazed by her transformation into a reliable schoolmistress, considering how sharp and sensitive she'd been before. Maybe having a foal had calmed her down, or perhaps it was the special relationship she seemed to have with James.

The girls kept a close eye on the weather forecast as they prepared for their riding holiday. Another low-pressure system moved through and then, as if by magic, a ridge of high pressure built over south-west England. It didn't look as if it would be moving in a hurry, either.

The morning they set off was perfect. A north-westerly breeze gave the sunshine a refreshing edge and kept all but the most determined flies at bay as Jacko and Max strode across the Common side by side, barely containing their eagerness to be off. They seemed to realise this was no ordinary ride.

"You know we agreed we should walk and trot because there's a long way to go?" Alice said.

"Yup."

"Well, a little canter up this stretch won't do any harm, will it? Just to the horizon."

"May help settle them," Katy agreed.

By the time she'd shortened her reins, Max had already accelerated into a flat-out gallop, powering over the purple heather, tail fluttering behind him like a flag. So much for a little canter! With soaring spirits, she leaned forward, lifting her weight off the saddle. It was all the encouragement Jacko needed. He surged forward, and Katy became lost in the familiar thrill of galloping, galloping, galloping . . . Impossible to think – just an awesome sensation of speed and elation. Galloping, galloping, galloping . . .

Eventually Max slowed to a canter, trot, then walk,

and Jacko caught up at last. Both horses were breathing heavily.

"Ahem! Little canter, my foot!" Katy said, laughing.

They grinned at each other.

"Seriously, though," Katy added, "I suppose we ought to take it easy. There's still a long way to go. Poor Jacko's got much shorter legs than Max."

So they walked and chatted, climbing higher and higher until they were on the broad, boggy backbone of Exmoor known as the Chains – an endless kaleidoscope of shimmering green, tinged purple in the sunlight, dusted here and there with tips of white cotton grass or, closer to the ground, spattered with bright yellow bog asphodel. From a distance the surface seemed like a soft blanket, but up close it was an ever-changing mixture: dark pools of peaty water, bright green mosses, lanky rushes and fan-shaped hummocks of spiky grasses. The safe areas of bracken and heather became fewer and further between as they pressed on, and finding a firm footing became increasingly difficult as they meandered between tussocks and around unsafe patches.

"The rain's definitely made everything soggier than I remember it," Katy remarked. She'd been sure she'd know the way, but any hint of a path had vanished, engulfed by new growth. She wished she'd concentrated more on the exact route they took when they went out on day rides with Melanie and Dean from Stonyford. It was too easy to follow like a sheep when someone else was in charge.

Alice became quiet and looked increasingly worried every time Katy glanced round at her. Even though Jacko was in front, trailblazing, Max was the one who frequently sank into the mire as its spongy surface gave way under his hooves. It wasn't simply his weight that was the problem, but the way he moved with long, decisive strides.

Jacko, on the other hand, had developed a classic native pony paddling action, probably learned from Trifle who appeared to be the world bog-busting expert. Quick, short strides meant each hoof touched down fleetingly, so it was almost impossible to sink – almost, but not completely, of course.

Katy's heart lurched as Jacko's shoulder suddenly dropped away underneath her. She let the reins slip through her fingers, freed her feet from the stirrups and held on to the front of the saddle as he plunged through the glutinous black liquid oozing through a flimsy crust of plants. "Watch out! Bog!" she heard herself shout unnecessarily. Granfer's advice would be to get off and remove the saddle as quickly as possible, to give Jacko the best chance of getting himself out, but all her instincts told her to hang on while he swayed and surged beneath her. And then, miraculously, the plunging stopped. She clung on to his mane, desperate to stay on board, while he hauled himself up onto firmer ground with a grunt and stood still, head down, legs shaking.

Oh, the relief! Katy noticed a broad tussock of grass and dismounted onto it. Her legs felt shaky too, and her heart was thumping. Jacko looked as if he'd been repainted, with dark legs, a dark underbelly and Appaloosa-type spots over the rest of his body. Looking down, Katy saw similar splodges on her clothes. Never mind, at least they were safe.

"What do we do now?" Alice called in a panicky voice.

With dismay, Katy realised they'd become stranded – Max on one side of the quagmire, Jacko on the other, and more boggy land to cross. Perhaps they should admit defeat and go back, but the ancient barrows that heralded better going were tantalisingly close, and if they accidentally took a slightly different route on the way home they could end up in an even worse predicament.

"Can you get off and lead him across?" Katy called back. At least Max would be lighter that way.

Alice leaned forward, as if preparing to dismount, but changed her mind at the last minute. "No! I don't think s-so!" She seemed to be paralysed by fear. "I really, *really* hate bogs!"

Max snorted and pawed the ground uncertainly, splashing away. The ground around him began to rock gently from the shockwaves.

Alice hit him on the neck, which was most unlike her. "Stop it!" she cried. "Oh dear. Please help!"

Somebody had to make a decision, and it clearly wasn't going to be Alice.

Katy ran Jacko's stirrups up their leathers, tied a knot in his reins, hooked them under a stirrup and told him to stand. This would put his horse agility training – standing still with his front feet in a hoop – to the test. Luckily, he seemed only too willing to stay put. His sides were still working like bellows after the exertion of getting out of the bog.

"Hang on! I'll come and get you!" she yelled, picking her way over a marginally drier route than the one Jacko had taken.

Before long she reached Max. He'd picked up on his rider's fear, and stood rooted to the spot. Remembering a tip from horse agility, Katy gently pulled him to one side so he had to take a step to maintain his balance, and that freed him up so he could move again.

Step by squelching step, they navigated their way back to Jacko, who was now looking to join them.

"Stand!" Katy had to remind him. "Stand!"

He fixed his eyes on her, and stood.

Max relaxed visibly when the horses were reunited.

Alice was still unusually quiet and tense. She looked close to tears.

Katy's socks and jeans were saturated with cold, peaty water. She could hardly get wetter or grubbier, so she decided to stay on the ground until they reached the barrows. That way she could walk in front, testing the ground. Vegetation could be deceptive, especially when viewed from above.

They had no choice but to go for it.

Although they had to double back on themselves a couple of times and take a detour around an old drainage channel filled with ominous-looking black gloop, they made it to the barrows and truly dry land in a matter of minutes.

They let the horses graze while they sat on one of the Bronze Age barrows and ate some chocolate to calm their nerves.

"Phew, that's better," Alice said, scrunching up the wrapper and putting it in her pocket. "I'd still be stuck out there if it weren't for you. I really was scared witless. Thanks for saving me."

Katy smiled. "Glad to be of service." She'd been worried – very worried – but not terrified. She understood only too well how Alice had felt, though. She'd experienced the same sort of mind-numbing, body-paralysing fear on the beach.

"I don't think I've ever felt like that in my life –

not before taking Viking into a big show-jumping competition or anything," Alice said. "Fear's such a peculiar thing, isn't it? What I was feeling a few minutes ago seems completely irrational now we're sitting on dry land with the sun shining and skylarks singing. Even that bog looks harmless from here. It's like waking from a bad dream to find everything's okay."

The rest of their ride was uneventful, although Katy's sodden jeans and socks made it less enjoyable than it would have been. She wished she'd put a change of clothes in her rucksack, but as the weather was good she hadn't bothered. At least the midday sun prevented her from getting too cold. Her jeans became increasingly stiff, like armour, as they dried out, and she got some funny looks from people when they were riding along the road.

They arrived at Mrs Soames' farm near Withypool at around four in the afternoon.

"Bought some ground?" she asked, looking amused. On Exmoor, falling off was known as buying ground.

Katy had been prepared for some sort of comment. "I had a voluntary dismount on the Chains," she said.

"An *honourable* dismount," Alice chipped in. "I'd still be up there if it wasn't for her."

"Well, I suggest we wash the horses down, check their legs and put them out in the field first. Those girths will need a good washing, too, by the looks of it. Then you can both have nice hot baths. I'll put the kettle on and ice the cake I've just baked, and when you're ready you can tell me all about your adventures over a cup of tea. If you want clean clothes, all your things are in the little trailer your grandfather brought over. It's outside the tack room at the moment. I'll tow it to the field for you after tea," Mrs Soames said, pointing towards the stable block.

Good old Granfer, Katy thought. He'd delivered the tent and everything else they'd need so they wouldn't have to carry it all.

The irresistible smell of baking wafted from an open kitchen window. Hot baths and freshly baked cakes weren't exactly what they'd had in mind when planning their back-to-nature camping holiday, but Katy wasn't going to turn either of them down. She remembered Granfer telling her that Exmoors shouldn't be blamed for being greedy – they were merely "opportunistic feeders". It was a very good survival strategy, apparently. Well, with a long, cold night in store, opportunistic feeding sounded like an excellent plan.

The conversation over tea had a decidedly boggy theme. Mrs Soames talked enthusiastically about notorious places on Exmoor: the Pinfords, Ducky Pool, Stranger's Allotment, Black Mires . . . There was "a particularly nasty though inconspicuous-looking one on Goosemoor Common" and "you could die out on Kittucks quite easily".

Alice stopped eating her cake and turned pale.

"Are there any bogs we should know about around here?" Katy asked.

"There's a splendid one near Landacre," Mrs Soames said, "but the nearest is up there." She pointed in the direction of Withypool Common. "On the moor between the road and Brightworthy Barrows – about a third of the way up. Definitely best avoided."

"Thanks. We'll steer well clear," said Katy.


It was nearly seven o'clock by the time Mrs Soames drove them to the field with all their belongings. She unhooked the trailer, bade them goodnight and left them to it.

They weren't alone for long. Jacko and Max soon came over to see what was going on, and seemed keen to "help".

"It's at times like this I wish we had unfriendly horses," Katy said, shooing them away from the open trailer.

"Let's pitch the tent near the stream," Alice said.

"Then we'll have an en-suite bathroom with permanent running water."

The tent was far larger and heavier than Katy had imagined. The label on the cover said *Four Person Deluxe*. Alice's family never did things by halves.

Katy spread out the tent's groundsheet, and Jacko immediately stood on it. "No, silly, this isn't a horse agility obstacle," she said, pushing him off.

He looked rather offended, and walked away swishing his tail.

Alice rolled the whole thing out and stared at the jumble of poles in the middle with dismay. "I thought I'd remember how to do this, but I don't. Mum's got it down to a fine art, so we always leave it up to her."

"Where are the instructions?" Katy asked.

"Lost ages ago."

"Oh." Katy picked up a few of the poles and studied them. She enjoyed doing jigsaws. The secret was finding a good place to start. Putting a tent together was bound to be similar. "Are the ends of the poles colour-coded?" she asked. "There are the same colours on the pole sleeves of the tent."

"Katy, you're a flipping genius," Alice declared. "Of course! I remember now."

Once they'd worked out the colour coding, it didn't take too long to thread the poles into their sleeves and fix them in place, lift the tent into position and secure the guy ropes. They even managed to match up the muddle of zips in the sleeping compartment without too much trouble. The in-built mosquito nets would be vital, especially as they were so near the river. Midges were already making their hair and bare skin prickle.

Alice produced a couple of large blow-up mattresses and a foot pump, and when she'd pumped them up they arranged their sleeping bags, fleecy blankets and pillows on top to make a cosy den.

"Actually, this is even more comfortable than your caravan," Katy said, snuggling down in her bed.

"Glamping, it's all the rage, da-arling!" Alice joked.

"You what?"

"Haven't you heard of it? Glamorous camping – *glamping* – camping with a touch of luxury." Alice rolled onto her side and rested her head on her hand. "So, what delicacy have we got lined up for dinner around the jolly old camp fire?"

"Baked beans with mini frankfurters," said Katy.

Alice snorted.

"And Mum's flapjacks for pudding."

"Ah, that's more like it. There's nothing more glamorous than a Barton Farm flapjack."

They lay in silence, looking out at the fading light through the half-open porch of the tent and listening to the stream, reluctant to move and get a fire going for supper.

There was another sound as well: rhythmic grazing and munching as Jacko and Max edged closer and closer. Katy was glad they'd decided to be in the same field as the horses. It felt as if they were all camping together, somehow.

"Oh, and there are apples for afters too," Katy said.

At that moment, Jacko and Max poked their heads through the front opening and looked around curiously.

"Apples? Did someone mention *apples*?" Alice said in a gruff voice.

Once the girls started giggling it was very hard to stop.

# 12

# Something Suspicious

"Laundry and egg delivery!"

The two girls surfaced from an unexpectedly deep sleep to see Mrs Soames peering in at them, holding a bowl of eggs in one hand and their clothes from the day before – washed, dried and neatly pressed – in the other.

"Wow, thanks," Katy muttered drowsily. From the light flooding in, she could tell it wasn't particularly early. She sat up, rubbing her eyes. "What time is it?"

"Eight o'clock, or thereabouts."

"Oh, sorry."

"Nothing to be sorry about. It's a beautiful day and I didn't think you'd want to waste it."

"Absolutely not," Alice said. "Thanks so much." After Mrs Soames had gone, she yawned loudly and added, "You can tell she's forgotten what it's like to be a tired teenager. We need to sleep in the morning – it's a scientifically proven fact."

Katy felt rather ashamed that Mrs Soames had needed to wake them. "I expect she'd milked a whole herd of cows by now when she was our age. Scientifically proven facts hadn't been invented then."

Breakfast was fried egg and bacon sandwiches washed down with mugs of tea. The eggs and bacon were crispy and peppered with ash because it was hard to adjust the temperature of an open fire. Alice tried to by pouring water on the flames, and nearly smoked them out.

They washed up as best they could in the cold stream, and then put tack on the horses and rode them up to the stables to feed them.

Mrs Soames offered them a cup of tea while Jacko and Max were digesting their breakfast, so they settled down at her kitchen table and plotted a route for their ride on the map they'd brought with them. Neither Katy nor Alice knew that side of the moor well, and after yesterday they were anxious to stay safe.

Lots of names came up that sounded familiar, yet

excitingly mysterious: Porchester Post, White Post, Molland Moor Gate, Lower Willingford Bridge, Humbers Ball . . .

Mrs Soames took her spectacles off and sat back in her chair. "That should keep you occupied for most of the day," she said. "Be back by mid-afternoon, though, won't you? Then I can take you to see Kestrel and his mares before we go to the pub for supper. My treat, by the way." She got up and went to the fridge. "Here, I've made packed lunches for you."

Katy and Alice put the packed lunches and the map into their rucksacks, thanked Mrs Soames and went to get their horses ready. They groomed them, sprayed on fly repellent, tacked them up, and set off up the farm drive.

Down in the valley, a group of stags lifted their heads to watch the riders heading towards Withypool Common.

It was impossible to feel anything other than happiness as they trotted over the sun-drenched moorland. Birds sang from every direction and fair-weather cottonwool clouds swept across the deep blue sky overhead. Two friends together, and a whole day to explore Exmoor on horseback. What could be better than that?

*

"Why don't we do this more often?" Katy asked as they stood outside the village shop, eating ice creams while Jacko and Max grazed the grass verge.

"Because we're usually too busy doing other things," Alice said.

Katy gave the rest of her cornet to Jacko. It was full of ice cream, and he curled his top lip upwards as he ate it. "Well, I think we should *make* time for things like this."

"Yes – it's been great, hasn't it?"

The day had gone much too quickly. They'd ridden through an amazing variety of beautiful countryside, from high moors to deep wooded combes, and had talked non-stop about all sorts of things.

"We'd better get going," Katy said. "Mrs Soames wants us back in good time so we can go and see her ponies. I can't wait to see Kestrel again."

"And his foals. I *love* Exmoor foals," Alice said. "They're the cutest baby animals ever."

Katy wondered, yet again, whether Dad was coping with looking after Simba. Now she knew what Mum meant when she said farmers were hopeless at holidays because they never stopped worrying about their animals at home.

The road between the village and Mrs Soames' farm took them over Withypool Common. Near the turning to the farm, a familiar-looking van was parked by the side of the road.

"I'm sure that's Dave's delivery van," Katy said.

"Yes, you're right," Alice agreed.

They spotted him crouched in the bracken some way down the hill. The stags they'd seen that morning were grazing peacefully in the valley, and he was watching them through his binoculars.

"Up to no good," Alice said in a half-whisper.

"He could just be taking photos. I think he's keen on wildlife photography," Katy replied, still wanting to believe the best of him.

"Hmm, shoots them with his camera and then his rifle, I expect," Alice said. "I really do think we should call the police."

"And tell them what? Deer-watching isn't a crime. Lots of people on Exmoor do it. He's not even trespassing; this is moorland, so everyone's got a right to roam here."

Alice sighed. "I suppose that's true, but it's so *frustrating*! That friend of his on the beach, the dog's pawprint on the Common and now this – there's something going on, isn't there? I'm sure of it."


When they got back, they told Mrs Soames. She was interested but not surprised.

"People round here have nicknamed him Dodgy Dave," she told them. "The police are pretty sure he's involved with poaching, but they can never get enough evidence to prosecute. Anyway, are we all set? I can't guarantee we'll find Kestrel, of course, but the whole herd was near the top at lunchtime. Trying to get some respite from the flies, I expect."

The ponies were certainly a long way from the road, over some extremely bumpy moorland. The vehicle threw them about like a bucking bronco; Katy hoped Mrs Soames knew what she was doing.

It would have been worth it just for the view, but luckily the ponies were there as well. Katy recognised Kestrel instantly. He was standing apart from the mares, but trotted towards them as soon as the vehicle came close.

"Can we go and take some photos?" she asked.

"By all means," Mrs Soames replied. "I'll stay here. They're more likely to run if there are lots of us."

Alice and Katy got out carefully and walked slowly towards Kestrel and his mares. Katy hoped they'd be able to renew the friendship that had blossomed at Exford Show, but he seemed aloof and wary.

"I'll go back," Alice whispered. "You'll have more of a chance alone. I'll take some photos with my phone."

"Thanks – mine's run out of battery," Katy whispered back. She'd kept her phone on the whole time and had taken lots of photos, and now there was no way of recharging it.

She walked in the general direction of Kestrel, but not straight towards him, keeping her imaginary flame low and focusing on the ground in front of her rather than the ponies. There was a group of six mares and a few well-grown foals with him, and they all stood their ground, staring at her. While they were still interested, she moved away again. She repeated the process, getting a little closer each time, and before the ponies knew it she was a few steps away. It was one of the mares, rather than Kestrel, who came up to investigate. She touched Katy's outstretched hand with her muzzle before backing away uncertainly, but she didn't flee. Kestrel, who'd been staring at Mrs Soames' vehicle, turned his head to look at Katy, and for a second his extraordinary eyes met hers. He does recognise me after all, she thought, eagerly reaching out to stroke him.

But she'd been too quick. He wheeled round, gathered up his family and cantered away down the hill.

She felt well and truly humiliated as she walked back to Mrs Soames and Alice.

"Don't take it personally, Katy," Mrs Soames said as soon as she'd sat down. "Out here on the moor he's got a job to do. His mares and foals are top priority and he won't be deflected from them – that's what makes him such a good stallion. I can never catch him out here, not even with a bucket."

Katy smiled at her gratefully. "He's got some lovely foals."

"Yes, he's done me proud. He'll be a hard act to follow. As I've said before, it's such a shame that filly of yours isn't a colt. Ah well, Kestrel will have a wonderful home with you. That's the main thing."

"I got a few photos, but now my phone's run out too," Alice said. "I brought my recharging lead without realising there'd be nothing to plug it into in a tent."

Katy sighed. "Me too."

Mrs Soames looked heavenwards. "The youth of today! Give me your phones, and I'll recharge them overnight for you in the house. It will be handy to have them for your ride home tomorrow. Then we'd better go and grab a table before it's too late. The pub's always ridiculously busy at this time of year."

Eating when you're really hungry is one of life's great pleasures, Katy decided as she scraped the last traces of mango cheesecake and ice cream from her bowl. They decided not to stay for teas and coffees because they'd already had so much and people were waiting for tables to become available. Katy was glad she'd soon be in bed; she felt weary all of a sudden.

As they drove back, they spotted a police Land Rover parked in a layby near the cattle grid onto the moor. Mrs Soames stopped and got out to see what was going on, and to tell them what the girls had seen earlier.

After what seemed like an age, she got back into the driving seat. "Deer poaching patrol," she said. "They're very grateful for your tip-off. Some of those stags in the valley have got magnificent heads on them, which makes them even more attractive, of course. Blooming poachers! They're causing no end of trouble." She ground the gears of the truck and moved off. "As I said before, we've all got a pretty good idea who the culprits are – some of them, at least – but the police need firm evidence in order to prosecute. Hearsay isn't good enough."

"What counts as firm evidence?" Alice asked.

"All sorts of things: blood can be DNA-tested, and photos of vehicles, tyre marks and even footprints can be useful. Oh, and catching them in the act, obviously," Mrs Soames added. "But that's easier said than done, and it's not advisable for the likes of you and me – things could end up getting nasty."

"Especially as they've got guns," Alice remarked.

"Even if they haven't. Apparently, some use dogs to bring the deer down instead of guns, and finish them off with a knife instead of a bullet. I suppose it's quieter, for one thing, but it's terribly cruel. Mr Wright reckons it may account for some Exmoor ponies straying recently, too."

Katy was horrified. "They don't hunt ponies as well, do they?"

"No. At least I'd be most surprised, with all the checks on horsemeat nowadays. But ponies are bound to get caught up with the deer every now and then, and the poachers often leave gates open for a quick getaway, which causes no end of problems – with farm livestock as well as ponies."

"Wow, you'd need a whole pack of dogs to bring down a full-grown stag, wouldn't you?" Alice said.

"Not necessarily. They use large, powerful lurcher types with African lion dog in them. Train them to run in front of their vehicles and follow the beam of the headlights to find their quarry."

"*Lion dog*?" Katy said, another puzzle piece clicking into place.

"More commonly known as the Rhodesian ridgeback in this country," Mrs Soames said. "We used to have lion dogs when we lived in Africa many moons ago. Lovely, loyal creatures, and formidable hunters. Originally bred to hunt lions, of course. They look rather like young lions, too, funnily enough."

# 13

# Bogged Down

When they arrived at the camping field, the tent looked like a deflated balloon. With loud exclamations, the girls rushed to inspect the damage. There were hoofprints all around, a couple of piles of fresh dung close by and several tent pegs had been uprooted, but no serious harm had been done as far as they could tell.

"Why can't horses leave anything alone?" asked Alice.

"I thought we might have been pushing our luck leaving them in here unsupervised," Mrs Soames remarked. "They're such inquisitive, playful creatures, especially geldings. Mares become more sensible with age, but geldings are nitwits for life."

The girls laughed.

"That's Jacko and Max – a couple of old nitwits," Katy said.

"At least we secured the tarpaulin over the trailer so they couldn't get at our food and their tack," said Alice. "I do hope Mum isn't cross about the tent, though."

Closer inspection revealed a rip in the flysheet and a snapped tent pole, but they mended both with some silage tape from Mrs Soames' truck and managed to resurrect the whole thing without too many problems. The horses came up to say hello and, finding they weren't particularly welcome, wandered off to graze nearby.

I bet they're secretly having a good laugh, Katy thought.

At last everything was more or less as it should be. Mrs Soames said goodnight and drove away.

Katy and Alice nestled into their beds, tired out after their long day.

"Alice?"

"Mm?"

"You know we saw Dave looking at those stags?"

"Mm."

"What if he was planning on going poaching tonight?"

"Police will deal with it."

"What if they don't? Should we keep watch, d'you think? It may be the best chance we'll ever have of catching him red-handed. He can't be allowed to get away with it – not after what happened to Simba." Katy was now convinced Dave had been involved.

"No way," Alice said firmly. "We can't go stumbling around Exmoor in the middle of the night, chasing after dangerous criminals. What would we do if we caught up with him or, most likely, *them*? Invite them back for beans on toast?"

Katy could see her point.

"Leave it to the police. They know what to do. We don't."

"You're probably right."

Alice yawned. "I know I am. Night night."

"Night," Katy said, but she was too anxious to feel tired now. Well, there was nothing to stop *her* from staying awake and watching out for the poachers, was there? Even down in the valley she'd be able to see their lights.

Alice was already snoring softly. With her sleeping bag under one arm and her pillow under the other, Katy crept out of the tent, found a tree to lean against and settled down. She felt rather like a stranded caterpillar as she sat in her green sleeping bag and peered into the silvery darkness. Stars glimmered in the sky.

The horses came up to inspect her and walked away again, grazing methodically.

Suddenly she was aware of other animals – dark shapes half hidden among the trees. One of them moved into a moonlit clearing on the opposite riverbank and came down to drink: the most magnificent stag she'd ever seen. His massive horns glinted in the moonlight as he lifted his head and looked straight at her, droplets of water falling from his lips. He must have known she was there, but still he drank some more before wheeling around and bounding back into the shadows. Four more stags came down to drink after him, and then, with a rustle of undergrowth, they left.

Amazingly, the horses took no notice of their field mates. Perhaps they'd been there all along. A barn owl screeched, reminding her of home. She thought about Simba, and Tinks, and Trifle. Then she remembered Kestrel, and imagined the lovely foals he'd have with her mares . . .

But after a while the sense of adventure she'd felt to begin with gradually gave way to boredom. Her head lolled uncomfortably against the rough bark of the tree. Mosquitoes were everywhere.

With her sleeping bag under one arm and her pillow under the other, she crept back into the tent again, zipped up the mosquito net and went to sleep.

*

"Katy! Katy! Wake up!" Alice was shining a torch in her face.

"What? Why? What time is it?"

"Around two o'clock. Listen, you were right. I think they're here!"

Katy tried to get her brain into gear, but it was fuzzy with sleep. "Who's where?"

"The poachers, of course! There are lights, and I can hear a vehicle – listen!"

Katy listened, and heard an engine revving somewhere further down the valley. A beam of light swept over the tent, dimly illuminating their bedroom and everything in it. Katy noticed that Alice was dressed.

There were rhythmic thuds as Jacko and Max trotted to and fro outside the tent, occasionally stopping and snorting with alarm.

*It's really happening!* Katy thought, fully awake now. "We should phone the police . . . Oh no! Mrs Soames is recharging our phones. D'you think we should go up to the house and try to wake her? We could phone the police from there."

"I don't think there's time for that," Alice replied. "What if they get away while we're up at the house? We ought to stay here and keep tabs on them."

"But we can't catch them single-handed!" Katy insisted. "We need help!"

"Hm, we need a plan of action," Alice declared.

"Like what, exactly?"

"I haven't got that far yet."

"Well, whatever we do we'll have to be quick," Katy said. "And we'll definitely need the horses. Let's tack them up while we make a plan."

"Good idea."

While Katy got dressed, Alice turned on her torch and rummaged around in the living area. "Here: hat and head torch. Don't turn it on outside unless you have to, though. They're bound to see it."

"Thanks." Katy adjusted the straps of the torch so it fit snugly over her riding hat and put the whole thing on her head.

The night air was cold and damp. Katy imagined Granfer saying "more haste, less speed" as she tried to saddle up Jacko quickly in the moonlight. First she got the reins and bit twisted round the wrong way on the bridle – something that never happened usually – and then the numnah slipped to one side when she did up the girth of the saddle and she had to start from scratch. He didn't help by fidgeting and blowing out his tummy.

Alice sat on Max, waiting.

"Why don't you go and wake Mrs Soames and call the police?" Katy asked, her fingers wrestling with the girth buckles. "I'll stay here with Jacko and keep an eye on the poachers."

"Are you sure you'll be okay?"

"Yes, positive."

"Promise you won't do anything stupidly heroic?"

"Promise. Hurry, though. If they set off and reach the road, Jacko will never be able to keep up."

"Alright, then. Bye! Good luck!"

"You too!"

Max's hoofbeats faded into the distance. Katy realised the engine noises had stopped as well. She could hear low voices somewhere in the valley, and faint patches of light filtered through the hedge at the bottom of the field.

She mounted Jacko. "Come on, let's see what's going on," she whispered.

They walked down the valley, following the river downhill. At the end of the field there was a gate in the hedgebank, so she made use of it to get a good view of what was going on. She couldn't see much, but maybe that was just as well. In the far corner of the next field she could make out a long truck and two men, lit by its headlights, bending over a large object. Close by, two dogs growled at each other, quarrelling over something they were eating.

She remembered the stag she'd seen earlier, and felt immensely sad.

The engine of the vehicle stuttered into life again and the beam of its headlights swung round towards her.

She pulled Jacko back from the gate so the poachers wouldn't spot her.

"Whoa! That'll do!" a man called in hushed tones. Bumping, banging sounds followed, and rather a lot of fairly loud swearing, from which Katy gathered they were loading what they'd killed into the back of the vehicle and it was unusually heavy, with large horns that got in the way.

At least the stag wasn't making it easy for them.

Without warning, Jacko turned his head and neighed loudly, presumably calling for Max.

"Hush, you idiot!" Katy whispered, but it was too late. Two dogs came bounding across the field, barking madly. She was just about to flee when a high-pitched whistle brought them to a standstill and they were called back to the vehicle. "Probably just a damned fool horse."

"Better get going, though."

"Yeah," Katy was relieved to hear them say.

Doors were shut and the vehicle turned again, presumably heading for an exit. Katy fumbled to open the gate in the dark before turning on her torch. Too bad if they saw her – the main thing now was to keep up.

Luckily, the gate opened and closed easily, and Katy cantered Jacko across the field, the beam of her head torch bobbing around all over the place. Pointing it where she wanted to go involved riding with her head down – not ideal for picking out a good route.

The rear lights of the vehicle were motionless, so Katy guessed the poachers had stopped at another gate. She urged Jacko into a flat-out gallop, and he responded enthusiastically. Although she couldn't hear anything apart from the pounding of Jacko's hooves, she knew the person who got out had seen her by the fact he ran back to the vehicle before it had driven through and he didn't stop to shut the gate afterwards.

Jacko had made up a lot of ground over the uneven field, but they were now on the smooth farm drive so the vehicle had the advantage.

They're going to get away! Katy thought desperately.

But at that moment a set of headlights turned off the road on the horizon and headed along the winding drive towards them. A blue light flashed above. The police had arrived!

The poachers had seen them too, of course. They came to an abrupt halt, shunted round and sped back towards Katy – no doubt intending to escape via the rough back track to the farm that the girls had used on arrival.

In the heat of the moment, Katy was tempted to stand her ground and block their exit route, but she knew it would be madness.

The headlights were getting closer now, dazzling her, so she guided Jacko onto the wide verge and prepared to witness the escape of the criminals she so desperately wanted to catch.

But the vehicle screeched to a halt, did a U-turn on the verge and veered away, heading for the gate onto open moorland that the girls had used that morning. For a split second Katy thought she must have magic powers, but then she noticed the more likely explanation: Mrs Soames was driving her truck down from the house!

Without the slightest hesitation, Katy followed the poachers. They were nearly at the gate, but showed no signs of slowing down. *Crash!* They drove straight though, leaving splintered timber scattered in their wake.

Katy picked her way through, anxious not to hurt Jacko's legs, and pressed on over the lumpy, bumpy and increasingly soggy moorland.

Behind her, the police Land Rover emerged slowly through the wrecked gate, illuminating the moorland with its headlights.

As the ground got boggier, Jacko gained on the vehicle; it crawled along, engine revving. Acrid smoke tainted the fresh air.

Katy realised where they were heading: to the bog that was *definitely best avoided* about a third of the way up the hill! She glanced back. The police were now following on foot.

*Sshrrumph!* With wheels spinning and engine spluttering, the vehicle sank deeper and deeper into the mire until it was submerged up to its door handles. What a stroke of luck – the poachers were well and truly caught!

Katy eased Jacko to a halt.

She'd had quite enough of bogs, even if they did have their uses.

## 14

# Foals and Friendship

Before the summer holidays ended, there was one more challenge Katy had to face, and it was the most daunting of all: discovering whether or not Simba would be lame for life. Would the pain and suffering she'd put him through be worth it in the end?

She would have liked it to be a private occasion, just in case there was bad news, but Simba had gained quite a fan club. Sharon, Dad, Mum, Alice, Melanie, Dean, Olivia, James, Granfer and Tom all gathered in the barn with Katy to hear Adam's verdict.

"Okay, let's make this as easy as possible for him,

and us," Adam said. "If you could put head collars and lead ropes on Jacko, Trifle, Tinks and Simba, we'll walk them around together. He'll feel much more confident surrounded by his friends. No high jinks, though. The idea is to keep him calm. We need to see whether his foot works properly as he walks. If it keeps knuckling over, like it did at the beginning, I'm afraid it will be bad news."

Katy wished he hadn't said that.

"For the moment, James, would it be okay for Katy to lead Trifle?" Adam asked.

James nodded.

"Good man. Right then, if Sharon has Jacko and Alice has Tinks – oh, hang on, somebody's got to lead Simba."

"I will," Dad said. "He knows me."

The amazement on Granfer's face was priceless.

Adam removed Simba's bandage and opened up his pen. "Katy, can you lead Trifle in front and let Simba follow? Take it very steady. And could everyone stand well back, be very quiet and breathe normally? We don't want him to be alarmed by anything."

Simba took a few steps, then froze.

"I expect he's been confined to his pen for so long that he's afraid to leave it," Adam said.

"He should face his fears like Simba," James said.

Katy smiled to herself. It was one of James' favourite

sayings, but it had never been more apt. "You're right, James, but he may need a little help."

Was Simba standing still because he didn't want to move, or was it because he couldn't move? Katy tried to keep calm. *Low flame, low energy, positive thoughts . . .*

While her attention was elsewhere, Trifle turned around and tried to walk into Simba's pen.

"Trifle! What on earth do you think you're doing?" Katy asked, embarrassed to have lost control so easily.

But now Trifle had got so far it was best to let her carry on and turn around in the pen. As soon as she was side by side with Simba, she stopped and touched muzzles with him.

It was then that Katy realised her clever pony was actually trying to be helpful. "Let's lead them out together, Dad, with Trifle slightly in front," she said.

"Okay. Anything's worth a try," he said doubtfully, but to everyone's astonishment, it worked! With Trifle leading the way, Simba walked by her flank, just as he'd walked with his mother during his early life on the moor. He was a bit unsteady at first, and shook his bad leg in the air a couple of times, but as he became more confident he began to walk properly.

Tinks, delighted to see the whole of her best friend at last, skittered along behind, so eager to play that

Sharon and Jacko had to form a barrier between the two foals.

They all looked at Simba intently, concentrating on the lower part of his injured leg, nobody daring to speak. It looked a bit odd for the first few strides – sort of stiff and hoppy – but gradually, as he walked, it got better and better and the foot was placed perfectly on the ground at every stride.

Eventually Adam broke the silence. "Well, I don't know what any of you think, but I'd say he's healed fantastically well. Obviously it's early days, and we must still be careful, but I couldn't be happier."

Katy felt like jumping for joy, but of course she couldn't. "Thanks for everything," she said to Dad.

He gave her one of his special smiles. "I never thought I'd say this, but I'm glad you were right."

They were so focused on Simba that no one heard the sound of footsteps approaching.

"Ha! Found you all at last!" Mrs Soames said. "Could have guessed you'd be playing with horses. Somebody left this coat in my car, so as I was passing I thought I'd drop it in."

"Oops! It's mine," Alice said. "Thanks so much! I was wondering where it had got to."

"Also, I thought you might like an update on the poaching saga. The police are delighted. All the evidence is there, from the carcass of the stag in the back of the truck to that dog with the damaged paw. They've been able to link those two crooks with a lot of other cases, thanks to you, and they're definitely going to press charges."

They all agreed that was brilliant news.

Mrs Soames gave Alice her coat. "Hello, cheeky monkey," she said affectionately to Tinks, and then came over to Simba. "Never thought I'd see you with an Exmoor, Phil," she remarked.

"Ah, this one's special," he replied.

"Certainly is," she agreed. "What a fine-looking fellow." She stroked Simba's neck and he turned his head towards her. "Friendly, too. Is this the one everybody's been talking about? The colt you rescued from the moor, Katy?"

"Yes," she said. "He's called Simba."

"You can see he's a Barton pony. They're so similar, aren't they?" she said, looking from Simba to Trifle and Tinks.

"Especially these three, because they're so closely related," Katy said. "Simba and Trifle have the same mum."

"Tormentil?" Mrs Soames asked.

"Yes, that's right."

"Well, this really is most exciting!" Mrs Soames said. "I think I may have found the stallion I've been looking for – if he's going to be for sale, that is."

156

"No, we could never sell him," Dad replied.

Katy looked at him in horror. What on earth was he doing? Mrs Soames would give him an ideal home!

"But I'm sure Katy wouldn't mind lending him to you," he added with a grin.

"Yes, we could do a stallion swap!" Katy exclaimed. "We'll have Kestrel and you can have Simba." She frowned all of a sudden. "Oh, but he's barely one yet, so he won't be much use to you next year."

"That doesn't worry me at all," Mrs Soames replied. "I like to give my mares a breather every now and again – a year off without a foal. Helps to recharge the batteries."

"It seems to me there's rather a lot to celebrate, one way and another," Granfer said. "How about making these ponies comfortable and retiring to the house for a drink or three?"

"Sounds good to me," said Mrs Soames.


As they walked down the hill to the farmhouse, Katy fell in step with Granfer and Mrs Soames. "I'm so looking forward to having Kestrel here," she said.

"And I can't wait to see Simba with my mares," Mrs Soames replied. "I have a feeling he'll give me the best foals ever."

"Apart from the foals Kestrel will have with my mares, of course," Katy said.

Granfer chuckled. "Do I sense old rivalries resurfacing?"

Mrs Soames grinned at him. "Absolutely. Foals and friendship – what could be better?"

"I think a toast will be in order," Granfer declared. "To foals and friendship!"

"And to Simba!" James shouted from behind.

"Yes, most definitely to Simba," Dad agreed.

"And to facing our fears like Simba," Alice said quietly, linking her arm in Katy's.

"Yes," Katy agreed. "Let's all drink to that."

# Author's Notes

This is the fifth book about Katy and her ponies. As usual, many people and ponies have helped me with my story.

Our Exmoor ponies – tame and not so tame – have provided me with endless inspiration for these stories about Katy and her ponies, particularly Nipper, Trifle, Tinkerbell and, more recently, Orion and Owly. If you'd like to find out more about our horses and ponies, and our farm, please take a look at my website, www.victoriaeveleigh.co.uk

Jacko was my first pony, and I loved him dearly. He

was a liver chestnut Welsh cob, and he was practically perfect in every way, just like Katy's Jacko. He's the only character I've ever taken from real life and put straight into a story unaltered, as I couldn't bear to change anything about him.

And Max? Well, he's rather like my friend Vanessa Bee's chestnut thoroughbred mare Secret, who's brilliant at horse agility.

Lots of friends and family members have helped me with this book in various ways, from being there when I needed them to providing me with ideas and reading through the first draft. It's impossible to mention everyone, but some deserve a special mention.

Peter Green is a very busy man, as he is an experienced equine vet as well as an expert in deer management. He gave up his valuable time to guide me through Simba's story and make it as realistic as possible, from the foal's initial injury to his treatment and the final outcome. In fact, Peter made it all so true to life that I found myself ringing him up with questions like, "Help! He still isn't drinking anything. What should I do?" or, "Poor Simba's getting really bored. Can't I let him move about *at all*?"

Both Peter Green and PC Martin Beck (our Police Wildlife Crime Officer) are actively involved in the campaign to stop deer poaching in our area, and they were very helpful when it came to the poaching storyline in this book. Between them they taught me a great deal about poaching and poachers, although I only used a fraction of what I learned in the actual story.

Deer poaching has become an important issue on Exmoor. It's a subject close to my heart because Chris and I love seeing Exmoor's wild red deer visiting our farm, and we hate discovering they've been taken. Unfortunately bogs are rarely there when you need them, but it was fun getting our fictional poachers stuck in one!

Tricia Gibson is a good friend and a talented photographer. She has been taking photos of Exmoor ponies for several years, and has built up a wonderful record of both free-living and tame Exmoor ponies. She kindly let me send one of her photos to Angelo Rinaldi for the front cover, and Chris also referred to her photos when he was drawing his illustrations.

It goes without saying that I'm incredibly grateful to my husband Chris for illustrating all my stories, including this one, and for putting up with strange meals – or no meals at all – while I was writing.

Fiona Kennedy, Fliss Johnston and the team at Hachette Children's Books have been helpful and supportive every step of the way. Fliss, especially, has provided me with encouragement and spot-on editorial advice.

If you'd like to find out more about Exmoor and its ponies, here are some useful websites:

Exmoor Pony Society
http://www.exmoorponysociety.org.uk

Exmoor Pony Centre
http://www.moorlandmousietrust.co.uk

Exmoor National Park
http://www.exmoor-nationalpark.gov.uk

Victoria Eveleigh
North Devon
December 2015

# Exmoor Ponies

Exmoor ponies are a common sight on the moorlands of Exmoor National Park in south-west England. Their distinctive appearance is one of the things that makes them so special; their bodies are various shades of brown with black points, and they have predominantly dark manes and tails and a 'mealy' buff colour on their muzzles, round their eyes and inside their flanks. There are no white markings on an Exmoor pony. For a few months during the summer they look sleek and glossy, but as winter approaches they grow thick double-layered protective coats to keep them warm and dry.

At a preferred height range from 11.3 hands (119cm) to 12.3 hands (130cm) the Exmoor is classified as a small British native pony breed. Its origins have become the subject of debate following recent research, but there's no doubt it's founded on the ponies that grazed the rough pastures in and around Exmoor for centuries.

The Exmoor Pony Society was founded in 1921, to establish and promote the breed, and to ensure the ponies were kept true to type. This was partly in response to a fashion for 'improving' ponies by using thoroughbred or Arab stallions.

During the Second World War, many ponies were stolen for food and fewer were bred. In the end, only about forty-six mares and four stallions were left on Exmoor. A remarkable lady called Mary Etherington encouraged some local farmers to re-establish their herds so that the breed was saved. Today numbers have increased to about 4,000 mares, geldings and stallions worldwide, but only about 500 of these are breeding mares that have had a foal in the past five years. The Exmoor pony is classified as a native breed at risk, and it's likely to stay that way due to its small gene pool.

Even though Exmoor ponies can now be found all over the world, Exmoor is still where most of the free-living herds can be seen. These herds fend for themselves for most of the year, but in the autumn they are gathered in by their owners so that the foals can be weaned and registered, the health of each pony can be assessed and the stallion can be swapped if necessary. The surplus foals that aren't needed as future breeding stock are usually sold to new homes at this time.

Taming a completely unhandled pony requires skill and patience, but it can be very rewarding.

If you'd like to find out more about Exmoor ponies, the Exmoor Pony Society has a very good website packed with information: www.exmoorponysociety.org.uk

A visit to Exmoor isn't complete without a trip to the Exmoor Pony Centre, near Dulverton. This is the headquarters of the Moorland Mousie Trust, a charity dedicated to the welfare and promotion of Exmoor ponies. For further details see the website www.exmoorponycentre.org.uk

The Trust runs a pony adoption scheme – the next-best thing to owning an Exmoor pony!